HOW to be a HUMAN

For Zulaykha Manye,
with lots of love

STRIPES PUBLISHING LIMITED

An imprint of the Little Tiger Group
1 Coda Studios, 189 Munster Road,
London SW6 6AW

A paperback original
First published in Great Britain in 2021

Text copyright © Karen McCombie, 2021
Illustration copyright © Thy Bui, 2021

ISBN: 978-1-78895-109-8

A CIP catalogue record for this book is available
from the British Library.

Printed and bound in the UK.

The Forest Stewardship Council® (FSC®) is a global, not-for-profit
organization dedicated to the promotion of responsible forest
management worldwide. FSC defines standards based on agreed
principles for responsible forest stewardship that are supported by
environmental, social, and economic stakeholders. To learn more,
visit www.fsc.org

MIX
Paper from
responsible sources
FSC® C020471

2 4 6 8 10 9 7 5 3 1

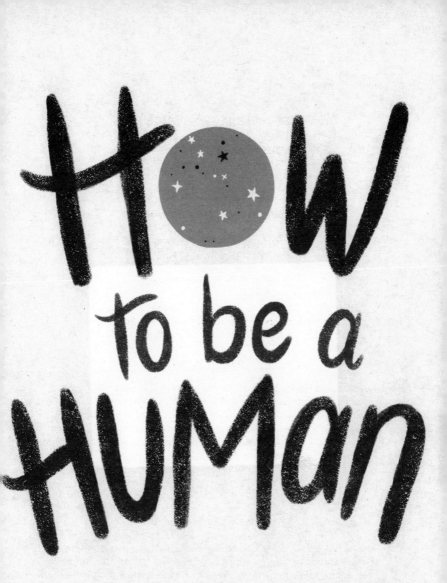

How
to be a
HUMAN

KAREN McCOMBIE

LITTLE TIGER
LONDON

The first storm

It came out of nowhere.

On the TV news, the cheery weather forecaster had predicted a fine, clear October night. But in the deep dark of the early hours, fierce cracks of thunder broke out – like granite cliffs exploding – and in rolled the storm. It startled the townspeople of Fairfield awake and sent them scurrying to their windows to see what was going on. In the brief hollows between booms, lightning fizzed and crackled and scarred the sky. The stars twinkled and twitched, blinking with the shock of it all.

House by house, flat by flat, lights and lamps flicked on till – *snap!* – the power cut plunged every building into darkness. The inhabitants bumbled about, searching for torches and candles, all clueless about what the town's river was getting up to. The meandering Wouze had suddenly swelled to twice its size and did what it had never done in its entire history … went walkabout. Up, up, up it soared, spilling over its banks, gliding across pavements and merrily gushing along roads. It seemed to want to know what the inside of buildings and houses looked like, sluicing through tiny gaps under locked front doors.

Then, as suddenly as it had started, the storm stopped, leaving the expanded river stranded. In that moment of calm, the power flicked back on, letting the stunned population of Fairfield get a good long look at the damage that had been done by the unexpectedly wild weather.

Outside, tree branches and For Sale signs swam alongside each other in newly formed streams.

Inside, occupants sloshed around in knee-high water, trying to rescue precious things, while pyjamaed teens and kids wowed in wonder at their river-soaked homes.

And far, far away – streaming through space – someone felt VERY guilty about what had just happened.

The damage
next day

KIKI: Fame and shame

Kiki's eyes flicked from the new posts on her phone to the breakfast news on TV. But it was still just some presenter blah-blahing about politicians arguing with each other. Nothing yet about the completely nuts weather in Fairfield last night.

"I'm not sure what time I'll be home from the hospital, Kiki," Mum called out from the hall, as she packed her nurse's uniform into her bag. "There's bound to be a staff shortage today with so many roads cut off."

"Hmm?" mumbled Kiki, all curled up on the sofa. In her lap was the TV remote, a plate of peanut butter on toast and her mobile.

She scrolled past an image of the usually neatly clipped grass of the park, which was now a shallow lake. It was lucky that her family's ground-floor flat was a little uphill, on the north side of town, so they'd escaped the worst of the weather madness. The torrential rain *had* slithered under the wafer-thin gap at the bottom of their front door, though, so that when Kiki first got up, the carpet had felt like spongy, boggy moss to bare toes.

"I said I'm not sure what time I'll get home!" Mum called out again.

Kiki heard her this time but was too busy scanning Snapchat for her schoolmates' storm stories to give a reply. Her best friends, Lola, Zainab and Saffron, all lived on the flatter south side of the river, close to school. Lola had just posted a pic of her living room, with water lapping at the bottom of her mega-screen TV and her sliders bobbing about like mini dinghies.

Zainab's post was of her excited little sister splashing about in the mud-coloured paddling pool that their kitchen floor had become.

Saffron messaged to say that she'd heard Harvey Wickes's gran had bodyboarded out of the front door of her flooded cottage, using a plastic sledge she'd dragged down from the loft.

(Disappointingly, there were no photos of that...)

"Kiki! Are you listening to me?" Mum asked, appearing in the doorway, jangling her door keys in her hand.

"Mmm, yeah ... I'm listening," Kiki muttered.

"Not sure if I'm entirely convinced by that," Mum said with a sigh, as she disappeared back into the hall. "But one more thing: Eddie's not opening his shop today, so he's going to stick around and help out here, which is handy, considering both your schools are shut."

Kiki rolled her eyes. Her six-year-old brother Ty was annoying enough – having Eddie as a sort of part-time nanny was like having an annoying big brother too. Eddie might be twenty years older than Ty, and have a qualification in electronics, but he was easily as goofy. He helped Mum out by looking after Ty a few days a week when she had long shifts. He shut up his repair shop early on those days and picked up Ty from school on a spluttering, ancient motorbike with a clattering sidecar, the two of them looking like something out of a kids' cartoon in their matching red crash helmets. It was mortifying.

"They should be back soon," Mum carried on.

"Unless they've drowned..." Kiki said under her breath.

Bright and super early this morning, Eddie had come knocking to suggest that he and Ty go and splosh round town in their wellies. It suited Kiki if they took their time; she was looking forward to having the flat to herself once Mum left for work, even just for a little while.

Settling herself even deeper into the comfy sofa, Kiki stared at her mobile – speeding through more storm-related posts – till her attention was snagged by the mention of a familiar name on the television.

"...in Fairfield, where a completely unexpected storm last night caused never-before-seen flooding in the town," said the newscaster, his silver-grey eyebrows bent into curls of concern as he sat in the comfort of the warm, dry studio. Behind his head was an inset image of Fairfield's ornate town hall, which was just a few minutes down the hill from Kiki's flat. The town hall's grand steps led on to what looked more like a harbour than a high street.

"Whoa..." mumbled Kiki, jerking to attention.

Without thinking, she put a foot on the floor and instantly winced as the wetness of the carpet seeped uncomfortably through her sock.

"Mum! Mum, come QUICK!" she yelled, at the same time trying to rescue the contents of her lap as the remote control, toast and mobile slipped sideways. "Fairfield's on the news – we're famous!"

"Really?" said Mum, reappearing in a flash. "What are they saying?"

Kiki waved her arms wildly to shush her.

"Our reporter, Lisa Garcia, is in Fairfield now," the newsreader continued. "Lisa, can you tell us more about this unprecedented incident?"

"Yes, thanks, John," said the young female reporter, who now filled the screen. "You may think I'm standing in the middle of a river, but it is in fact the town's main street."

Kiki noticed that Lisa Garcia looked nervous. Then she spotted the problem: little waves of floodwater were slapping and slurping over the top of the reporter's red wellies.

"There's not a soul in sight here, John. Clearly, everyone is busy trying to deal with the catastrophe that hit their homes in the early hours," Lisa carried on professionally. "Except, hello ... I've just spotted someone! Hi, there!"

The reporter beckoned someone off camera to come closer. From the left, a boy awkwardly sploshed towards her, his knees playing peek-a-boo in the gap between his skater shorts and wellies. Even though it had stopped raining, the boy had the hood of his black Puffa jacket pulled up. A tuft of white-blond hair peeked out from under it, above his round pale face.

"Can I ask your name?" said Lisa, flipping the microphone towards the boy.

"Wes," said the boy, blinking madly as he leaned in too close to the mic.

"So is your school shut today, Wes? Has it been badly flooded?"

Lisa tried to move the mic away so he wouldn't foghorn into it again, but the boy just leaned closer.

"Yes," he said, peeking out of the hood.

Lisa hesitated for a second, hoping for more, before realizing she wasn't going to get it.

"And what's the name of your school?"

"Riverside Academy."

"Ooh, he's from Riverside!" said Mum. "Do you know him, Kiki?"

"He's in my year, but I don't really *know*

him," Kiki replied, flapping her arms again to shut Mum up.

Kiki didn't really know many of the other Year Sevens. She and her old primary-school friends, Vic and Megan, didn't even speak to each other any more. Within a week of starting at Riverside, Kiki had found herself scooped up by the Popular Crew. That didn't go down too well with Vic and Megan, and when they'd overheard Kiki describing them as "just some girls" she "sort of knew" from primary school, it had been the final straw. Vic and Megan had never forgiven her and had found a new crowd to hang out with. Kiki could hardly blame them. She'd have done the same if it was the other way round.

But as she stared at the boy, Kiki realized she *had* noticed him around in the corridors, constantly blinking or drumming his fingers on some book or other, and always, *always* being shouted at by passing teachers to take his hood down and "get that jacket off".

"The storm was short but savage." Lisa persevered with her interview. "It must have been pretty terrifying to witness?"

"Er, not really," said the boy. "I was watching *Star Trek Beyond* on my laptop and fell asleep with my headphones on. So I missed it."

Kiki burst out laughing, then started frantically messaging Lola, Zainab and Saffron.

Switch on the news – you have GOT to see who they're interviewing from our school... #TOTALGEEKALERT!

She paused for a second, wondering if the hashtag was too mean. But then it was the sort of thing Lola would say, so surely that made it OK, didn't it?

"EXCUSE ME!" came a high-pitched yelp from the TV. "*I* saw what happened!"

"Oh my goodness, Kiki!" gasped Mum. "It's your brother – it's Tyreke!"

Kiki looked up at the screen again.

Both Lisa and the hooded boy had swivelled round. They were staring at a young boy behind them. He was floating past the town-hall steps on an inflatable flamingo, wearing a red crash helmet and waving a lightsabre.

"It was ALIENS! I watched them out of my bedroom window!" Ty shouted.

"Oh no," mumbled Mum, slapping her hands to her face. "Not *this* again..."

"They were zooming around in SPACESHIPS that were like GLOWING DODGEMS doing LASER QUEST!" blurted Ty.

"Noooo!" groaned Kiki.

Kiki's brother was an expert fibber. His lies were legendary. All his friends still stared down at Kiki's feet whenever they saw her, even though she'd *twice* taken off her trainer and SHOWN them that she didn't have an extra toe. And the trusting little gang absolutely believed that Ty's part-time childminder, Eddie, had a secret government lab in the back of his dilapidated electrical repair shop, when all Eddie *actually* did was fix people's toasters.

As for Mum, her pioneering brain surgeries kept her very busy (she was a nurse in A & E), and Dad wasn't around because he lived in a lighthouse (he'd moved out a year ago to a flat above a photocopying shop in Birmingham).

When the storm woke him in the night, Ty had a shiny *new* fib to tell. He'd run between Mum and

Kiki's bedrooms, yelling that he'd seen tiny neon-yellow spaceships zigzagging across the blackened sky.

And now here he was, on national TV, blabbing his spaceship fantasy to the whole country. Kiki and Mum swapped glances, united in weariness at Ty's unstoppable habit of telling tall tales.

"Ha! So there we have it," said the reporter, turning back to face the camera with a wry smile. "Last night's storm and flooding were caused by aliens. It's official! Back to you in the studio, John."

"But it's TRUE!" roared Ty, as a pair of rangy arms – belonging to Eddie – reached in, grabbed the back of the inflatable flamingo and dragged it out of shot.

Lisa stared at the camera and held on to her rigid grin.

The hooded boy stared at the retreating flamingo and its rider.

The screen switched back to the newscaster in the studio.

And Kiki felt her blood run cold.

Please, please, PLEASE let none of my friends have seen that, she thought frantically.

PLING

And *there* it was, the message that mattered most. The one from the Queen of the Popular Crew. Lola.

OMG, Kiki. Is your little bro for real? ALIENS! Own the shame, friend! #hahaha

Whenever school started back, it would be way too soon to live this down.

In that second, Kiki wished a stray spaceship would beam her up and speed her away to *wherever* wasn't here.

Friday:
the night
he came

KIKI: Everything unravels

Three weeks after the storm took it by surprise, Fairfield was getting back to normal. Schools had reopened, the River Wouze was meandering where it ought to be and, best of all, Lola's house had dried out, been redecorated and was party-ready for Friday night.

And now Kiki stood outside Lola's glossily painted front door and tried to wish and squish away the nervy butterflies in her stomach. She was running late. *Was everyone else here already?* she fretted. *Would she know anyone besides Lola, Zainab and Saffron?* Lola had mentioned she'd invited some of her old friends, who'd gone to secondary school in the neighbouring town.

Then again, Harvey Wickes and his mates Jake,

Jarek and Archie went to Riverside and *they'd* be here. Kiki wasn't sure about them though, they were always so loud and cocky. But maybe she just needed to get to know them better. Maybe they'd be fun.

"Come on," Kiki ordered herself. With a shaky finger, she pressed the doorbell and heard the deep *bing-bong* announce her arrival.

She shivered, glancing up at the early evening sky. The autumn sunshine had gone and the wind had whipped up, with fat, bruise-coloured clouds jostling each other for space. Mum had nagged her to wear a coat but Kiki hadn't wanted to cover up her costume and ruin the effect. Now she looked down at the DIY outfit she'd put together and her heart sank. Her Rey costume suddenly looked like what it was: hastily home-made. The bandages wound round her arms – soaked in coffee to get the right colour – were still damp and threatening to unravel.

Whatever, Kiki reassured herself. *It'll be OK. It'll be a laugh.*

She struck a pose, flicked on Ty's borrowed lightsabre and took a selfie before ringing the doorbell again.

WES: A churning of clouds

Wes hadn't exactly jumped for joy about school starting back, but he'd punched the air when Dad mentioned that the chip shop on the high street was reopening.

Clutching their Friday night tea of fish and chips, Wes paused for a second in the opening of the alleyway, rummaging around in his pockets for his inhaler. Up ahead was the side entrance to his flat, but hurrying back from the chip shop had made him wheezy, the sudden violent wind practically snatching his breath away.

At last his fingers found the blue plastic tube and he gave it a shake – it was nearly empty. He'd have to remind his dad again about registering with a new GP... Their old medical practice was miles away, in the village they'd moved from in the summer.

With one hand clutching the hot paper package to his chest, Wes leaned his back against the brick wall and took a shallow gulp of what was left of his meds. As he waited for them to do their work, he let his gaze drift up to the chimneys and roofs of the houses opposite – and frowned.

Something about the light had changed, and not *just* because he was in a bin-lined dark alley. A churning of clouds in a shade of sickly green hunkered above the town like a rumpled, lichen-coloured duvet. And tiny flickers of lightning seemed to dart *within* the clouds, Wes noticed, as his own eyes darted to keep up with them.

Then *another* sudden flicker of light caught his attention – one closer to the ground. The torch-like beam came from the direction of Lola whatshername's house, directly across the street. He recognized the tall, skinny girl standing on the doorstep, even with her normally springy dark hair pulled back into a tight bun at the nape of her neck. She was one of Lola's best buddies. There were four of them, always swanning round the corridors at school together, acting all cool. But the girl looked more nervous than cool right now. *And why was she dressed as Rey from* Star Wars? Wes wondered to himself, watching as she struck a pose with the lightsabre, then awkwardly let it drop down by her side.

When he'd popped out to the chip shop ten minutes ago, he'd seen a bunch of girls he didn't recognize from Riverside. They'd gone tripping into Lola's, all giggling and glammed up, with stupidly tiny backpacks over their puffy, fluffy jackets. This girl *definitely* didn't look like one of them.

Still, the mystery of the Rey lookalike wasn't nearly as fascinating as what was going on in the sky. Wes tilted his head back to watch the strange weather again. Then, in an effort to get a better view, he tilted his whole body, not realizing that the lid of the curry sauce tub balanced on top of the bundled chips had come loose.

"No!" he yelped, as the hot liquid oozed down the front of his jacket.

KIKI: Wars versus wears...

Kiki turned at the sound of the yelp and saw the weird kid Wes – the one who'd been on TV after the storm – nearly drop the package he was holding, before lurching into a funny hop, skip and juggle as he caught it again. A second later, he scuttled off down the alley and disappeared into the gloom, just as Kiki heard the front door finally swoosh open behind her.

She switched on a smile as bright as her brother's lightsabre and turned back to face her friend.

"Are you kidding me?!" shrieked Lola, standing in the doorway dressed in a turquoise vest top, black leggings and with a temporary rose tattoo on her shoulder.

Kiki's heart sank somewhere below the soles of

the too-big, knee-high, brown leather boots her mum had lent her.

"You ... you're not in fancy dress," Kiki said in surprise.

"Of course I'm not!" Lola replied, with a what-are-you-on-about shrug of her shoulders.

"But at lunch break you said it would be fun to come as someone from *Star Wars* tonight," Kiki muttered weakly, as she flicked off the lightsabre.

"Ha!" Lola snorted, breaking into a broad grin. "I said we should dress like we're in *Star WEARS*, you idiot!"

Star Wears, Kiki repeated in her head as her blood ran ice-cube cold.

Of *course* Lola had said *Star Wears*. Lola, Zainab and Saffron were obsessed with the reality fashion show where celebs styled regular people with clothes from their own showbizzy wardrobes.

"Hey! Check out Kiki, you guys!" Lola called out as she padded back into the house, her shiny dark hair swishing with every step, her box-fresh white trainers bouncing along the newly laid carpet in the newly painted hall.

Kiki hesitated – all she really wanted to do was turn

and race back home to change into something sane.

Or maybe Lola could save her...

"Could I borrow a top and jeans?" she whispered, as she trailed awkwardly after her friend.

"No way!" said Lola. "This is too funny!"

Lola carried on along the hallway. There was nothing for it – Kiki would just have to brave it out. But any bravery she might have felt trickled away as soon as she walked into the huge, open-plan living room and kitchen at the back of the house and saw the sea of unfamiliar faces. The tidal wave of laughter that hit her full in the chest didn't make her feel any better.

Kiki scanned round desperately for a sighting of Zainab's colourful hijab and always perfect winged eye make-up, for Saffron's piled-high bun and chunky black glasses. But when Kiki finally spotted them, their laughter was just as hard and harsh as everyone else's.

Still, they seemed to be making their way over to her. Maybe one of them could rescue her with a linked arm or a best-mate hug?

"Just one word – WHY?" Zainab asked when she got close enough. Her nose crinkled in disgust, as if

Kiki smelled like she'd slept in a bin overnight.

"It's a mistake, OK?" Kiki babbled quickly, feeling like she was practically *steaming* she was so hot with embarrassment. "I thought Lola said—"

"You thought Lola said you should make the biggest idiot of yourself?" Saffron joked. "Well, you did it! You won the prize, girl!"

Lola, Zainab and Saffron. Her so-called best friends. Couldn't even *one* of them help her out here?

"Back in a minute," Kiki mumbled, turning and hurrying out of the room.

"*She's* the one I was telling you about," Kiki heard Saffron say to whoever.

"OMG! The one whose kid brother said all that mad stuff on TV about aliens?" she heard the person say, followed by *more* laughter.

Kiki sped up, the soles of her loose-fitting boots sinking into the deep pile of the cream carpet as she hurried up the staircase, heading for a hideout.

With a reassuring *thunk*, she locked the bathroom door behind her and stood there for a second, shocked and silent. In the quiet of the cool room, she heard a low rumble of thunder outside, which perfectly matched her mood.

Saffron's right. I am a prize idiot, she thought miserably.

How could she fix this? How could she make this awful evening even the tiniest bit more bearable? Kiki glanced round, and spotted the silver bin by the loo. A flutter of an idea came to her: if she got rid of the bandages on her arms – since they were already unravelling – what she was wearing could NEARLY pass as normal.

Taking a few steps towards the bin, Kiki quickly tugged off the loosening cloth – then caught sight of herself in the mirror above the basin.

"Nooo...!" she yelped with a pained wince. Coffee stains zigzagged all over her bare arms. Grabbing a fistful of toilet paper, she wet it under the tap and started scrubbing at her skin.

"Please come off, *please!*" Kiki muttered, as a rattle of the door handle was swiftly followed by an impatient thumping.

"Oi! Hurry up!" a boy's voice yelled.

"Use the toilet downstairs!" she called back.

"Nah – there's a queue. Come on!"

With a sigh, Kiki threw the bundled toilet paper in the loo, gave it a flush and unlocked the door.

"All right, Chewbacca?"

It was hard to make out Harvey Wickes, since he was waving her brother's lightsabre around in front of him. The plastic tube clunked against the wall, and Kiki winced, wishing she hadn't left it out on the landing. Her brother had only lent it to her as long as she promised to take *excellent* care of it. If she took it home dented, Ty would never forgive her.

"Give it to me, Harvey," said Kiki, holding her hand out, trying to sound more fearless than she felt.

"Nope. No way," said Harvey, taking a step back. "Not till you say please."

"Please," Kiki said wearily.

"Louder!" Harvey demanded, enjoying her discomfort.

"PLEASE!" she repeated, through gritted teeth.

Harvey narrowed his eyes, contemplating ways to torture her more.

"Say it in Wookiee," he finally said, with a grin that was more of a sneer.

Kiki gave him a death stare. Harvey's version of having a laugh was clearly all about laughing *at* people.

"Look, please, just—"

"Sorry, but no Wookiee, no lightsabre!"

Clenching her fists as well as her jaw, Kiki tried to think what sort of noise a two-metre-high alien furball would make if it was asking for its brother's favourite toy back.

"Aaaa-EEEE-oowwww-whoooo!" she yelled, feeling her face flame hot. She held out her hand.

But Harvey seemed to have lost interest in humiliating her. He was staring past her at something in the bathroom.

"Uh-oh... Lola! LOLA! Come quick!" he shouted, dashing over to the bannister. "Your toilet's gone mad!"

Kiki turned to see what he was making such a fuss about – and watched, horrified, as the water in the loo overflowed, spilling over the tiled floor and out on to the landing.

Something had clearly blocked the toilet and, with a sense of growing dread, Kiki realized what it was.

"No, no, no!" she whispered, picturing herself lobbing the bundled loo roll into the toilet bowl – along with the crumpled bandages that were meant for the bin.

"What's going on? What's happened?" she heard Lola shriek, as she rushed up the stairs and spotted the mini waterfall coming from the bathroom. "OMG ... Mum and Dad are going to *kill* me!"

Kiki didn't suppose saying sorry was going to be enough, either in English or Wookiee.

WES: The something in the sky

Standing on wobbly tiptoes on his bed, Wes reached up to hook the plastic clothes hanger over the curtain rail. He'd managed to sponge the curry sauce off his jacket, and if he kept the window open a bit, it should be dry by morning, especially with the wind buffeting it about.

Job done, Wes was about to step down when a sudden microsecond blast of sheet lightning illuminated the figure of the tall, skinny girl-who-was-Rey in the street below. She was now hurrying *away* from Lola whatshername's house, her lightsabre bobbing in her hand.

But that wasn't all. Wes jerked as he spotted a movement in the sky. Something seemed to have *burst* from the bottom of a cloud, causing wisps to whirl and twist after it, as if the 'something' was tumbling towards the ground. Except there was nothing to see.

"Whaaaat...?" he muttered, as a momentary glint, a shimmer of yellow, flittered into view and then vanished. From the tantalizing glimpse he'd got, it had looked like an object or a piece of debris that was flying – or falling – very fast.

A grin slowly spread across Wes's face. Most of the time, his life was pretty beige, with all the bright colours saved for the sci-fi series, gaming and graphic novels he loved so much. But right now, it felt like he was watching a *genuine* UFO event framed by his bedroom window!

Wes knew it couldn't *really* be true, but there was no harm in imagining...

KIKI: Crushed

Turbo-fuelled by sheer embarrassment, Kiki ran.

She wasn't aware of bursting clouds high above her as she bolted from Lola's house and hurried down the road that led towards the Wouze.

Turning on to the riverside path – the school grounds on one side, the mud-swirled river on the other – Kiki slowed to a miserable stomp. But still she didn't notice the dotted street lamps spluttering and flickering above her head, electricity humming and zinging in their posts ... didn't feel the rain soak her home-made costume till it stuck to her skin ... didn't see the plastic advertising banner attached to nearby railings ripple and flap itself free in the strong winds. It twisted and tumbled backwards over the wire school fence and into the head-high tangle of bushes in the lower playground.

With her confidence crushed, and tears of shame blinding her eyes, the only thing Kiki wanted was a hug from her mum. She took her mobile out of her pocket, about to call and ask her mum if she could walk down the hill and meet her, and then thought better of it. By the time Mum had wrangled fidgety Ty into his rain things, Kiki could be back at the flat, and curling up on the squashy sofa with Mum and a hot chocolate.

As the cringy memories of the evening came flooding back, Kiki quickly deleted her stupid Rey selfie from Instagram, relieved to see it had no likes or comments yet.

That crucial task done, she tilted her head back and ROARED her frustration out loud, her screams swallowed by the wind and rain, her lit-up lightsabre waving angrily – and uselessly – in the face of the storm.

STAR BOY: Crashed

The Star Boy stood a little unsteadily in the middle of the large open area between low buildings, his thin amber-coloured skin shocked by the never-before-felt sensation of pattering water droplets.

He looked up and down his smooth, spindly body, quickly examined his long, gangly arms and legs, and was relieved to see that nothing was obviously broken or torn. His hands ached a little, but when he held them up and tried moving the main paddle shape of each one, what Humans would call 'thumbs', he realized the ache must have come from gripping the controls fiercely tight as his pod tumbled from the sky.

But there was something else. The data that normally ran in his left eye had vanished – the lens must have dislodged on impact.

Flicking his eyes rapidly to and fro, he did his best to scan the scene:

- *dark, large clump = some kind of plant life*
- *pod in the middle of it = plant life cushioning the impact*
- *damage to pod = unknown, but invisibility shield still operational*
- *damage to automatic location alerter = unknown*
- *smoke trailing from damaged pod, but endless sky water eliminating it almost immediately*
- *location and invisibility of pod + eliminated smoke = pod should remain undiscovered by Humans*
- *must locate shelter*
- *must locate recharging opportunity.*

An immense flash of sheet lightning made the Star Boy pause in his assessment and glance up. How startling it was to be staring at the sky above, instead of being a traveller gazing down!

And, of course, travellers and observers were all he and the Others were ever meant to be. The Master had been furious with them after the last study voyage they'd undertaken. As they'd headed back to their planet, he'd bellowed at his students through their earpieces: hadn't he instructed them to just watch, learn and leave? Hadn't he drilled it into them that they were NOT to impact on the environment of Earth and NOT risk being spotted by Humans? Fooling around – shooting laser bolts and darts to deliberately set off storms – was not acceptable.

He'd informed them that they'd have to undertake the voyage AGAIN at a later date, and this time do it properly and carefully, or they'd *all* fail the module.

The Star Boy hadn't joined in with the previous risky behaviour. But he was part of the class and had to accept the class punishment, and so this evening he found himself in the middle of the school fleet, travelling in formation, pods about to be set to invisibility mode, ready to properly study this randomly selected spot on the alien planet of Earth.

He didn't know which of the Others broke rank first, but his hearts sank when he saw the first sharp glint of a yellow beam hit a barely there drift of vapour, turning it into a rolling, expanding, grumbling storm cloud instead.

After that, the bolts and darts escalated. The Others were so lost in their idiotic behaviour that they didn't spot the stray bolt that collided with the Star Boy's pod. No one noticed as he went hurtling Earthward, his pod's control panel suddenly blank and unresponsive, including the communication device. He'd frantically swiped and swiped again at the panel. And when the weak, juddering orange light of the invisibility shield flicked on, he felt only a second's worth of relief, till he realized he didn't even know if he and the pod would survive the impact of the crash, invisible or not.

Now, as the Star Boy gazed upward, the night sky instantly dimmed and stilled. With sinking hearts, he knew all too well what that meant. The Others were gone, recalled by the Master, who'd have been observing the voyage remotely from the Education Zone and seen it go disastrously wrong once again. Who'd have ordered his students to return before the storm escalated and became as devastating as the last one.

It was good news for the Human settlement of Fairfield, of course, but it didn't help the stranded Star Boy. All he could do now was keep himself safe.

Taking a few stumbling steps sideways, the view beyond the plant life revealed itself. Criss-crosses of wire made some sort of barrier that he could see through, and beyond this wire barrier was the gushing snake of river he'd spied from above. When the stray bolt hit, the Star Boy had been certain his pod would hurtle straight into the river's terrifyingly murky, unknown depths. But then he'd steered hard and managed to avoid it. Just.

Though where *was* here?

A flapping sound close by caught his attention. He lifted a corner of the long, thin item – made of some kind of slippery material – that was draped across the bushes. Human words were printed on it, he noticed excitedly. He had studied many, *many* Earth languages for the fun of it, including:

- *Mandarin Chinese*
- *English*
- *Hindustani*
- *Arabic*
- *Malay*
- *Russian*
- *Yoruba*
- *Latin*

and the two large words he was deciphering were most definitely the ancient language of Latin!

"Terra firma," he said aloud, and felt instant hope. Because *terra firma* meant 'solid ground'. It was a good omen. There were other words and symbols alongside the phrase, but before he attempted to decode them, all three of his pulses suddenly began to race. There was a figure on the other side of the wire. Not close, but close enough to be worrying, especially when he saw that it was waving what appeared to be some kind of *weapon*. The white haze of it swung menacingly through the air in a figure of eight.

The Star Boy stumbled and slunk into the bushes, watching.

But the figure wasn't watching him. Instead, it carried on stomping along the path beside the river.

It was a Human, obviously. A Human *Girl*, he decided.

Everything will be fine, he reassured himself, holding still to quieten his pulses.

"Terra firma

Terra firma

Terra firma..."

As he chanted his new, calming mantra, the Star Boy didn't realize that his rain-filled black eyes and basic translation skills were not *quite* good enough to decipher *and* understand all the lettering on the long, flappy item he'd found.

Hurry to the Terra Firma Flooring sale NOW - 30% off everything! Offer MUST end soon!

But interpreting a plastic advertising banner for a cut-price carpet showroom was the least of the lost alien's worries. He scanned the terrain, looking for a place to hide and, more importantly, one where he could recharge. It would be unfortunate to survive the crash only to expire from lack of electricity...

The first
weekend
on Earth

KIKI: The sticky-tape spaceship

Easing herself awake, Kiki yawned and stretched her arms above her head, luxuriating in Saturday-morning-no-school deliciousness.

Until a niggle began to stir in her sleep-addled brain ... and the whole messy, squirmingly awful disaster of last night's party came back to her.

When she'd got home, Kiki had held back from crying, waiting till Mum got Ty out of his bath and into bed. Then she'd sat and sobbed on the sofa, telling her mum about the shame of her *stupid* costume blocking up the *stupid* toilet, while Mum provided hugs, understanding and lashings of tissues. Something had stopped Kiki telling her mum about the meanness of her friends, though – a weird kind of loyalty to Lola, Zainab and Saffron.

She could hear Mum's muffled voice now, her words indistinct. The one-sided tone of it meant she must be on the phone. Maybe it was Dad checking in for a chat, like he did every few days. Then an awful thought came to her: maybe it was Lola's parents asking Mum to pay for the damage Kiki had caused!

Dread changed to panic. Kiki flipped up on to her elbow and reached across with her other arm, snatching her mobile from the bedside table and checking through all her platforms.

Nope, nothing. No reply from Lola to any of the twelve **I am SO sorry!** messages she'd pinged. No reply from Zainab or Saffron to the handful of **Do you think Lola will forgive me?** DMs.

Kiki stared at the screen, her thumbs poised, wondering if she should try messaging again...

"VOOOOSHH!"

At the sound of the sudden roar, Kiki sat bolt upright. The next moment, her bedroom door swung open and her brother barged barefoot into the room, holding something high in the air with one hand.

"Ty ... get out," Kiki said wearily, propping herself up on her pillow. "I don't need this right now."

"Yeah, but look what I made, Kiki! VOOOOSHH!"
Ty roared some more.

"What's it even supposed to be?" Kiki asked,
squinting at a contraption made out of a plastic
milk carton, star-shaped glittery stickers and a lot
of sticky tape.

"It's a SPACESHIP, of course!" said Ty, his PJs a
blur of tiny multicoloured dinosaurs.

Kiki couldn't help squinting at the carton as it
cruised by her face. This close, she could see that
a wonky windscreen had been cut in the front of
the plastic, and something, probably one of her
brother's smaller soft toys, was stuffed inside, acting
as an intergalactic test pilot.

"Look, just go," Kiki growled, trying to wave Ty
and his milk carton away.

"Ooh, that looks impressive, Ty!" said Mum,
appearing in the doorway.

Kiki narrowed her eyes. Mum seemed calm and
smiley. She didn't look like she'd just had a difficult
conversation and demands for cash. Kiki let her
shoulders relax a little. She let them relax even
more when Mum mouthed, "You all right?" at her
over the top of Ty's head. She gave Mum a sort of

shrug in reply.

"Is it a plane?" Mum asked Ty.

"No! It's a SPACESHIP!" Ty roared, as he galloped around. "And I'm going to paint it BRIGHT YELLOW, so it's the same colour as the REAL alien ones I saw in the properly BIG storm last month!"

When Kiki had walked, soaked and soggy, into the flat yesterday evening, she'd found Ty in a sulk, having missed the burst of weird weather because he was in the bath. By the time he'd scrambled out, the skies were calm and there wasn't an 'alien' to be seen.

"Speaking of storms," said Mum, "I was just on the phone to Lucas's dad, sorting out Ty's playdate later, and he said that lightning struck an oak tree at your school, Ty. It fell on the roof!"

"REALLY?!" Ty squeaked in surprise.

"Yes, really!" Mum said with a nod.

"I bet there's a HUGE hole in it!" Ty said excitedly, crash-landing his spaceship on Kiki's duvet. "Me and Lucas can check it out THIS AFTERNOON when we're trying out his new DRONE!"

Kiki pictured comfy old Fairfield Primary, nestled beside the park – and her comfy old friends,

Vic and Megan. Back in the early summer, they'd sat on a bench in the park after school, staring across the Wouze at Riverside Academy, wondering what secondary school had in store for them.

Back then, the three girls had never heard of Lola. They didn't know Kiki would be in the same form as her, and that Lola would suggest she come and hang out with her and Zainab and Saffron one lunchtime – with one lunchtime turning into every lunchtime, every breaktime and after school every day. They couldn't have imagined that Kiki would be so flattered to be included in the Popular Crew that she'd totally turn her back on her old buddies and get caught saying clunky things, making out they'd never been that close.

Every time Kiki was in the park, she'd look over at the bench and feel prickles of sad and sorry.

"Well, that's fine, as long as Lucas's dad is OK with it, Ty," Kiki vaguely heard Mum chatter.

But Kiki's attention was suddenly grabbed by an alert trilling from her mobile. With a surge of hope, she stared at the screen. It was Saffron! Kiki quickly skimmed the message – and instantly wished she hadn't.

Hey, Kiki. Me and Lola and Zainab all had a talk and decided maybe you need to hang out with other people from now on. OK?

OK?! Kiki repeated silently to herself. *How could that be OK?*

"Kiki? Kiki?"

It took a second before Kiki realized Mum was talking to her.

"Was that Lola?" she asked.

"It was Saffron, not Lola," Kiki answered vaguely.

"Uh-huh," Mum muttered, clearly not wanting to ask too much about her friendship issues while Ty was bouncing around. "Are you all planning to meet up later, as usual?"

There it was: that funny edge to Mum's voice, the edge she always used when she mentioned Lola and the girls. The reason Kiki hadn't included them in her teary moan last night.

Kiki had only had her friends round to their flat once, and Mum hadn't exactly loved the comments Lola had made about how small it was – and how freaky Ty was. She was far too polite to say so out loud, but Kiki knew her mum wasn't exactly keen on Lola. And, right now, Kiki wasn't particularly keen on Lola and her other friends either.

"Um, no – we're not meeting up today. Everyone's a bit..." She wanted to say 'mean', but decided not to. "They're a bit busy."

"That's a shame," said Mum, sounding not at *all* sorry. "Maybe you could call someone else?"

Who? thought Kiki. Who exactly did Mum or Lola and the others think she could hang out with?

Of course Mum was talking about Vic and Megan, but hanging out with them again was never going to happen. She hadn't told her mum how she'd treated them. She was too ashamed of herself to do that.

"Do you want to come and see if the tree's DESTROYED my school, Kiki?" asked Ty. "I'm sure you can have a go with the drone!"

"No thanks," Kiki said flatly, but Ty had already scampered out of the room, leaving the spangly milk-carton spaceship dumped on her duvet.

"Aw, you are such a kind and thoughtful boy, Ty!" Mum called after him. "Isn't he a sweetheart, Kiki?"

Kiki didn't answer. She was too surprised by what she'd just seen on her bed.

"You reckon?" said Kiki, raising her eyebrows as she pointed at the hand-made spaceship.

It took Mum a moment to realize what Kiki was trying to draw her attention to, which was a wild-eyed hamster squeezing itself out of the plastic milk-carton windscreen while retching over Kiki's favourite bedding.

"Oh my goodness, Squeak!" yelped Mum, gathering up the confused and vomity hamster.

Disgusting as it was, Kiki couldn't help thinking of all the aliens usually depicted in books, TV shows and films. Instead of mysterious, glowing, otherworldly beings, what if they were actually only ten centimetres high, round, fat and furry?

Kiki almost smiled, till she remembered she'd just been firmly friend-dumped...

STAR BOY: Into the Outside

Thwack-thwack-THWACK!

It happened in a nanosecond. A creature – waving two wide spans of feathery folds – hurled itself at the window.

The Star Boy leaped backwards, terrified it was going to come crashing through the glass and career into the low dark room that had been his refuge since his own crash the night before.

But, none the worse for his ordeal, the creature landed effortlessly on a ledge by the window, tucked the feathery folds neatly into its side, and instantly became small, round and recognizable.

"Coo! Coo-coo!"

The Star Boy's racing pulses began to settle. It was a bird – one of the plump grey ones he'd been watching this morning as they strutted in the Outside, tapping their pointy noses at the ground. He wished he had his data lens so he could identify which type of winged Earth creature they were.

"Coo! Coo-coo!" the grey bird repeated, tilting its head and staring at him quizzically from the other side of the glass.

The Star Boy smiled at the strange language the bird used. *What was it trying to communicate to him? And what other noises might he hear in the Outside?* he wondered.

So far, he hadn't dared leave this hunkered-down room he'd found at the bottom of a building, which had turned out to be useful in more ways than one. It was dominated by a large metal box with a sign on it that read DANGER! HIGH VOLTAGE! in bold red letters. In the dark of the night, the Star Boy had gratefully renewed his energy from it. And in between healing blasts, he'd stared out of the small, dusty window – his inky-black eyes at ground level – marvelling at how the dark sky lightened and brightened, slowly, gently, softly changing colour. On his planet, there was no night and day, only constant electric brightness, time marked simply as flagged alerts on his data lens.

And as the wondrous Earth day dawned, the Star Boy's concerns about being stranded faded away. For the last few peaceful hours, he'd looked in amazement at things he'd only heard about from the Master during Earth Studies:

- *birds*
- *sunshine*
- *clouds (puffy)*
- *clouds (ripply)*
- *clouds (thin and stringy)*
- *planes*
- *tiny, buzzing insects.*

An urge to be in the Outside suddenly gripped him, the thrilling notion of using *all* his senses and not just sight. What did clouds smell like? Could he taste sunshine? What would it be like to stroke an insect? Perhaps he'd catch a glimpse of a Human!

Also, now that he was stronger and renewed, he knew he should get to his pod and assess the damage. Crucially, he needed to see if the location alerter was operational, so that a rescue craft could find him. Just as crucially, he had to hunt for his missing data lens.

First things first. Walking away from the window, the Star Boy stopped by the room's metal door, pressed his fingers over the locking device and focused his kinetic energy. After a dull clunk and a sharp, satisfying click, the mechanism came free, and the Star Boy opened the door by its handle, just as he'd done on the *opposite* side the night before.

Now in the cool of the Outside, the Star Boy warily glanced around. He was standing at the bottom of a space that contained the metal door, the window and ledge where the bird sat, and six steps that led up to ground level. He'd counted them when he fell *down* them in the dark yesterday evening.

Good – the glance confirmed to him that there were no Humans nearby at this present time. But he wasn't taking any chances – the Star Boy and the Others had heard enough warning stories from their Master about what alien beings on other planets might do to them if they were ever captured during one of their Educational Excursions. They could find themselves being tested like an experiment, locked away forever or even evaporated.

His skin rippled with worry at that thought, then

just as quickly rippled with the exciting, wafting tingle of Earth air, and the knowledge of what he was going to do next. Holding himself very still – and trying to remember what he'd been taught in class – he began to pause his pulses, noting his amber glow fade ... until he was *entirely* invisible. Only then was he brave enough to walk up the six stone steps into the complete openness of the Outside.

As he made his way over towards the rustling, towering greenery where his pod lay hidden, he pushed aside a nagging concern about what he was doing. Pulse-pausing caused *serious* depletion of energy, he knew, and he had no idea how long he'd have before his own dipped dangerously low and his invisibility faded. (They hadn't covered that module with the Master yet.)

But with a quick, reassuring check back at the open metal door and the DANGER! box in the gloom of the down-below room, the Star Boy moved forwards, his moment's doubt swirling away at the magnificent sight of a few grey birds unfurling their feathery folds. They spiralled from the ground into the air as he approached – clearly *sensing* his presence if not actually seeing him – before landing not very far away and resuming their pointless, pointy-nosed tap-tapping.

They must be hunting for food, he decided, though how exactly they could find any on this flat, stony terrain, he had no idea. Unless tiny pieces of stone were part of their diet? Or plants, perhaps, he thought, spotting one particular bird pecking at the base of some low-growing vegetation.

Curious, the Star Boy bent over, determined to discover what a round grey bird might eat for a meal.

Seeming to sense the tiniest movement in the air as the Star Boy came close, the bird agitatedly trotted backwards and forwards, as if it was defending its patch, not wanting to share the titbit it had found.

If the Star Boy's pulses weren't already stopped, they would have at the sight of the tiny, fragile, glinting thing that the bird had been pecking at. A tiny, vital piece of tech. His missing data lens!

Without wasting a second, the Star Boy scooped it up and placed it firmly where it belonged, in his left eye, and was immediately rewarded by an instant tumble of incoming information:

- *bird species = pigeon*
- *feathery folds = wings*
- *pointy noses = beaks*
- *terrain = tarmac*
- *large green plant life = bushes, or a shrubbery*
- *low-down vegetation = daisies*
- *sudden, sharp, piercing pain in eye = a substance called grit, found randomly on Earth's surface.*

But as he sifted through the data, the Star Boy was disturbed by a strange, non-bird, non-insect, metallic-sounding humming. Still frantically blinking away the grit, he glanced up at the sky, trying to locate the source of the unknown sound, but could see nothing.

Walking round the towering green mass of shrubbery he found himself at the criss-crossing wire fence that ringed the area. Placing his hands on the cool mesh, the Star Boy gasped at the daylight sight of the fast-flowing river beyond, at the narrow bridge that spanned it and the disordered jumble of many, many brick buildings on the far side, their wonder hidden from his view in the dark of the previous night-time.

ZZZZZZZZZZZZZZZZZZZZZ

The insistent buzzing hum drew the Star Boy's attention away from the startling view of the Human settlement.

He glanced up, his eyes locking on to a small machine hovering in the sky. The data in his lens ran fast, quickly identifying it as a kind of flying recording machine. A drone. A camera.

Without pausing to think, the Star Boy went into survival mode, flicking his hand to send a fine, light-speed bolt zapping into the sky, halting the humming machine in its tracks. The drone tipped in its orbit and toppled, flitter-fluttering earthward – or possibly riverward.

But the Star Boy didn't wait to find out. Light-speed bolts drastically drained energy, and his supplies were already compromised by the previous few minutes of exploring the terrain while unseen. He desperately needed to get to safety, recharge and become his glowing true self again.

Veering back across the tarmac towards the sanctuary of the down-below room (a basement), he felt flooded with two sensations:

• *fear that he was so very nearly spotted by a Human camera contraption, and*

• *guilt over possibly destroying some prized possession belonging to a Human.*

Thwack-thwack-THWACK!

OOF!

Both the Star Boy and the pigeon were momentarily startled by their mid-playground collision. Who knows what the bird made of bouncing off thin air, but it reminded the Star Boy that he was, in fact, invisible – so the small flying camera in the sky wouldn't have seen him anyway.

A third sensation washed over him:

• *how very stupid he was, as the Master always liked to remind him.*

Monday:
How to spot a Human

KIKI: The shimmering surprise

Kiki spent the weekend holed up in her bedroom, staring at her mobile, wincing at the photos Lola, Zainab and Saffron had posted. For the last few weeks that they'd been friends, Kiki would have been in photos like these, all four of them pouting on the town-hall steps, posing in the changing rooms in H&M. *This* weekend it had just been three.

And now it was Monday and Kiki would have to face them at school. While Ty ran back inside the flat for the fourth time to collect yet *another* something he'd forgotten, Mum turned to Kiki as they waited by the front door.

"Look, I know you're dreading today, Kiki, and obviously what happened at the party was humiliating," Mum said, squeezing Kiki's shoulder.

"But I'm sure it'll be just a funny story by this morning."

"Don't think it will," grumbled Kiki, feeling the knot in her stomach tighten.

Mum leaned in and gave her a hug.

"Well, just walk into school with your head held high, and be ready to laugh along with any teasing," she suggested, rubbing Kiki on the back.

Kiki thought of Lola's silence, of Saffron's very final-sounding message, and doubted she'd be laughing much today.

Then the hug was over, and Mum was checking her watch.

"I have to go or I'll be late. But I'll be thinking of you today, Kiki, and keeping my fingers crossed," she said.

With a shout goodbye to Ty, she hurried off.

"BYE, MUM! BYE!" yelled Ty, finally tumbling out the door.

Kiki turned the key in the lock and turned her brother to face downhill.

"What's wrong with you?" Ty asked, as they set off to Eddie's.

"Nothing's wrong," Kiki replied flatly.

"Are you cross cos it's Monday and YOU'VE got to go to school and I don't?" said Ty, waving his lightsabre and trailing after his sister.

Fairfield Primary was closed till the damage caused by the fallen tree could be assessed. Much to Ty's disappointment, he hadn't managed to get an aerial view of the roof of the school at the weekend. The drone had dropped out of the sky almost as soon as it was launched, and had only *just* missed falling in the river. At least Ty had been useful and taken Lucas, his dad and the broken drone to Eddie's shop to get it fixed.

"Nope, I'm not cross about that," said Kiki, speeding up.

"But you look VERY grumpy, Kiki," Ty continued, skipping and hopping to keep up with his sister. "Like you've swallowed a WASP."

"I haven't swallowed a wasp, Ty," said Kiki, as calmly as she could, hoping she could avoid this conversation getting stupid, which was a distinct possibility with *any* conversation involving her little brother. She noticed Ty was wearing his jacket the wrong way round. It matched his brain, really.

Kiki quickly steered Ty across the road, towards

a row of faded-looking shops directly opposite. Eddie's shop was nestled between the Busy Bubbles laundrette and Mr Pickle's minimarket. Just as Kiki and Ty set foot on the pavement, the front door of the Electrical Emporium was yanked open.

"Hi, guys!" Eddie called out, dressed in his uniform of band T-shirt and jeans, a lopsided smile on his pleased-as-a-puppy face.

"Kiki's swallowed a WASP!" Ty announced, as he hopped and skipped up to Eddie.

"Wow, have you?" Eddie asked Kiki, as gullible as ever.

"No," Kiki answered firmly and she turned and quickly began to walk away. "By the way, Mum says thanks for babysitting Ty today, Eddie."

Eddie's "No problem!" drifted behind her as she stomped down the hill.

A couple of minutes later, Kiki came to the junction with the high street. She crossed over, taking the lane that led to the pedestrian bridge across the Wouze. On the other side of the river was the grotty view of the back of the school, home to jungle-like shrubs and a smelly collection of big metal rubbish containers.

As she set off along the riverside path – in the wake of other students scurrying to the entrance round the corner – a memory of stumbling along this very same path on Friday night suddenly settled on her shoulders like a soggy blanket. But there was nothing for it: she'd just have to walk into the playground and face the long, hard glares of the girls who didn't want to be friends with her any more.

Unless, unless... Her eyes flickered over to the wire fence that separated the riverside path from the lower playground. One panel looked a little bashed and ripped, as if something had clattered into it. Kiki hurried over and pushed the wire mesh experimentally. It gave way.

With a squash and a squeeze, Kiki wriggled through the gap and was officially on school grounds. Now she had to carefully wend her way through the head-high bushes she found herself in before she could take refuge by the smelly bins till the school bell rang.

Carefully pushing through the slapping branches, she shoved a long tangle of plastic signage out of her way. And then something made her hesitate, a gleam off to her left in the heart of the towering shrubs. Something was shimmering, glimmering ... silvery yet with a hint of acid lemon.

Pushing aside the bobbing purple heads of a butterfly bush, Kiki stared at this completely unexpected and out-of-place whatever-it-was. It looked like a great metallic egg, as big as a small car. *But was it made of metal?* she wondered. It seemed to shudder ever so slightly in the breeze.

Apart from what it was made of, what on earth could it be? Perhaps it was a science experiment that had served its purpose, floating away from a teacher and landing out of sight here. Or maybe it was some kind of creative-writing prompt. Maybe she'd turn up to English class later only to find Miss Amari leading all the students back out to see the exciting 'alien' landing, before telling them she wanted a short story, a news report and a haiku written about it by the end of the week.

Kiki automatically went to grab her phone out of her pocket to take a photo, but the sound of the school bell stopped her.

BE-ZINGGG! BE-ZINGGG!

Wriggling her way out of the bushes, Kiki stepped into the empty lower playground.

Only it wasn't empty.

WES: That being-watched feeling...

Technically, the lower playground was out of bounds to students, but Mr Shah, the site manager, made an exception for Wes.

The first time he'd caught him sitting on the steps that led down to the basement boiler room, Mr Shah had spotted the *Doctor Who* graphic novel he was holding and, instead of telling him off, he and Wes got into a friendly debate about who the best Doctor Who monster or villain was.

Ever since, in good weather, Wes had happily sloped off with his latest library book to his personal reading corner at breaktimes and lunchtimes. Mornings too, if he arrived a bit early like today.

The only other living, breathing creatures he ever saw there – apart from Mr Shah and the occasional lunchtime staff member dumping leftover food gloop in the bins – was a random scattering of pigeons.

But this Monday morning Wes had the strangest feeling he was being watched. Twice.

The first time was just as he'd been studying an awesome illustration of an Ood. He heard a thin, high-pitched whine coming from *inside* the basement and froze, keeping his eyes fixed on the page – glad of his hood to hide in – too scared to turn his head in case he came face to face with something or *someone* in the small boiler-room window.

The whine stopped, his panic ebbed away and common sense took over. *There were* always *random mechanical noises burbling away in the basement*, Wes reminded himself, calming his overactive imagination.

And then he heard *another* noise.

Not a soft, high-pitched whine this time, but a loud, low groan coming from the direction of the bushes.

He closed his book and stood up. Rooted to the spot, he watched as branches and leaves twitched and shook.

There was something in there.

It's OK, it's fine, there's got to be a rational explanation, mumbled the sensible part of Wes's brain. *It could just be a pigeon. A pigeon with a really deep coo.*

IT COULD ALSO BE AN OOD! the frantic side of his brain interrupted.

Wes hovered, suddenly uncertain if he really *wanted* to see an alien now that one might be very, very close.

But what burst out of the undergrowth wasn't a deep-voiced pigeon or an Ood. It was a fed-up-looking girl. The girl who was Rey, who had run away from Lola whatshername's house in the storm on Friday night.

"All right?" she said, brushing leaves off her blazer.

Wes tried to respond, but a gulp of awkwardness was lodged in his throat, and all that came out was a gurgle.

STAR BOY: Specimens and skills

The Star Boy hadn't meant to let out a whine.

He had been relaxing, recharging, leaning against the metal DANGER! box, when he'd heard the familar "Coo-coo!", and gone hurrying over to the basement window to look for his pet pigeons.

But his smile had changed to the high-pitched whine of shock as he approached the window. There, in the dense shrubbery, he'd observed the faint, shimmering glint of his pod! He'd been baffled, recalling that yes, the invisibility shield had malfunctioned for a moment after he'd been hit by the stray bolt and tumbled to Earth, but it *had* been in perfect working order since the crash. His mind had raced, realizing he'd need to get out and attend to it as soon as possible.

And then the Star Boy nearly whined *again* as his attention was grabbed by something spectacular. A Human – a completely still Human – was sitting on the steps! Rippling with excitement, the alien quickly paused his pulses so that he could safely – and invisibly – put his face close to the window to examine the specimen. It was male but young, he decided. But how old exactly? All he could remember in his excitement was that Humans lived for a short time compared to his own kind. He scrolled quickly, trying to estimate the Human Boy's age, and settled for around twelve years old.

As for his clothing, the Human Boy wore some kind of black padded material on his body that also covered most of his head. He was staring down at a block of paper in his hands. A 'book', the Star Boy realized. But this reading activity was puzzling to him; why did the Human turn the pieces of it so slowly? Why did he not simply flick through it in nanoseconds and source all the material at once?

With a sudden *snap!*, the Human slapped his book shut and stood up. The Star Boy saw the Human's strangely pale face, as round as the Earth's moon inside a black, shiny circle of fabric, and wondered at the expression upon it. What did it signify? The Star Boy's knowledge of Human emotions was limited; it was not a major focus of the Earth Studies his class had undertaken.

And then he understood that it must be surprise, or perhaps alarm, because – and the Star Boy could hardly believe his luck – a Human Girl had just materialized from the green mass of the large plant life! With a jolt, he recognized her, though her body coverings were different. He'd seen her soon after his crash-landing, striding along by the river, waving a weapon; though on reflection he realized it had simply been a kind of illumination device.

But, recognition aside, the Star Boy felt a surge of panic – had this Human *Girl* spotted his damaged pod nestled in among the shrubbery? Hopefully not, he decided. Logic indicated that she would also be wearing an expression of surprise or more likely alarm on her face, or that she would have instantly told her fellow Human of her find.

Instead, he watched in fascination as the Human Boy mounted the steps and the two creatures stared uneasily at each other. Surprisingly, they barely used words. In fact, their communication mainly consisted of staring and then grunting at each other, after which the Human Girl walked away. *What had that exchange meant?* the Star Boy wondered.

A thought hit him...

While he was here – awaiting rescue – he could do something no one from his planet had *ever* done before. Instead of sourcing information about Human lives and customs and earthly marvels from the satellites that littered the Earth's atmosphere, instead of watching from afar on Educational Excursions, the Star Boy was here, now, and could observe Humans up close. He could film them and collate reports on their behaviour. He would be hailed as a scientific hero by the Master when he returned to his planet!

And if he *was* to do that then why not start with THESE two particular Humans? The tall, skinny Girl and the shorter, moon-faced Boy.

Yes, he would do it, he decided, excitement sparking from him as the specimens hurried away.

The Star Boy just needed to think about *how* he could track them. He could hardly follow them directly: he didn't know where they'd be going, he couldn't pause his pulses indefinitely, or be too far from his comforting, life-saving DANGER box!

Suddenly it came to him. In an attempt to impress the unimpressible Master, the Star Boy had already begun to study the modules on Spying Skills that would be taught next term: the art of directing senses along electrical pathways (Channelling) and the art of taking on the shape of other entities (Morphing).

He would test out what he knew of Channelling, the Star Boy decided, turning and staring at the electric cabling that ran off into the walls.

He walked over to the DANGER! box and placed his hands on it. He concentrated, running relevant Channelling data in his lens, at the same time trying to recall all the information he'd already absorbed.

And then – with a fizz and a jolt – it began. His senses instantly zipped and tore through the cables, being conducted at breathless speed through the school buildings, all packed with many, many young Humans whom he could hazily see in his mind's eye. Off his senses whizzed again, careering into computer systems, shooting along wires tucked in walls and ceilings, seeking and searching out his two *particular* Human specimens...

KIKI: Stutters and sparks

Breathless, late, Kiki hurtled into the first class of the day – and stopped dead as she found her usual seat taken. She looked around the table at Lola, Zainab and Saffron, but they deliberately avoided her gaze, as if swapping her for a bewildered boy called Bilal was perfectly normal.

But almost instantly, Kiki realized that it was in fact a very clear message: she was not forgiven.

"Let's get going," Mr McKenzie, the music teacher, said, waving Kiki to Bilal's usual spot.

With all eyes on her, Kiki sat down. For the next fifty minutes, the endlessly enthusiastic Mr McKenzie tried to get his students excited about Holst's *The Planets*, blasting out the classical music, accompanied, of course, by a dull PowerPoint of static images of planets.

And for those endless, awkward fifty minutes, Kiki desperately tried to ignore the looks, sniggers and whispers directed her way. Her gloom grew as she realized that *everyone* knew about Friday and what had happened.

"Pssst, Kiki," hissed Will, who was sitting opposite her. "Did you dress like this for a dare?"

Kiki glanced at the phone screen he was holding up – and saw herself posing outside Lola's front door, the coffee-stained bandages around her arms making her look more like a mummy than a *Star Wars* warrior.

The dawning realization that someone had screenshot her post before she'd deleted it made Kiki's chest heave with dread. Her whole body prickled with embarrassment as she pictured the image being passed round her year group and beyond.

She looked away, studiously staring at Mr McKenzie. Even then, from the corner of her eye, she caught glints of phone screens being surreptitiously shared. She heard Mr McKenzie endlessly shush the whispers and sniggers that kept breaking out.

After spectacularly failing to 'laugh along with the teasing' as Mum had suggested, Kiki was finally released from the torture by the end-of-lesson bell. Chairs screeched and the sudden chitter-chatter was so loud that Mr McKenzie could barely be heard reminding them all about homework.

Kiki hesitated, letting everyone – especially Lola, Zainab and Saffron – shuffle out of the classroom ahead of her. As she stood there, Kiki felt herself deflate, shrinking under the weight of her public shaming.

"Everything OK, Kiki?" Mr McKenzie's voice cut through her misery. Kiki always thought his New Zealand twang made everything he said sound bright and hopeful – exactly the opposite of how she felt right now.

"Yes ... fine," she lied.

There was the hint of an I-don't-quite-believe-you frown on Mr McKenzie's tanned forehead, but he didn't push the point any further.

"Actually, I wanted a quick word," he continued.

"But I'll be late for geography," Kiki mumbled, desperate to be out of there now in case he saw the tears that were threatening to fall.

"I won't keep you long," said Mr McKenzie, his back to the whiteboard, where a paused image of Saturn's rings haloed his head of scruffy fair hair. "I just wanted to mention our practical sessions. I've noticed you always opt for the xylophone?"

Kiki had no idea where Mr McKenzie was going with this, but she couldn't help picturing herself half-heartedly clonking at the wooden bars. Lola said playing a musical instrument was totally lame, that the *best* thing to do was to do the *least* you could get away with while rolling your eyes and yawning.

"I'm just mentioning this because, back at the beginning of term, didn't you tell me that you were pretty good on the ukulele?" Mr McKenzie carried on.

"Uh, maybe," Kiki replied.

She'd learned to play in primary school and loved it so much that Dad had turned up for one of his visits with *her very own uke* in a cute carry case with a rainbow strap. But as soon as she'd started hanging out with Lola she'd stuffed it under her bed, where it lay forgotten.

"It's the school's Open Evening on Thursday,"

said Mr McKenzie.

Kiki gave a so-what? sort of shrug, even though she'd loved attending the Open Evening for new students last year with Mum. Over the course of the visit, she'd tried out experiments in the science department and eaten rainbow-iced cupcakes in the food-tech room.

Best of all was the head teacher's talk in the crowded hall ... not because of Mrs Evans' never-ending speech, but because of the three Year Seven musical acts that had played straight after. Kiki watched in awe as a rock band, a boy on Spanish guitar and duetting girls performed on the impressively huge stage, bathed in professional spotlights.

"That'll be *you* this time next year, Kiki! Up there with your ukulele!" Mum had said, giving her a nudge and a smile.

Kiki had beamed back then, imagining that chance to come. One year on and she couldn't think of anything worse.

"Well, how would you feel about performing after Mrs Evans' speech?" asked Mr McKenzie, as if he'd read Kiki's mind and wanted to torture her.

"We've got a rap band, a saxophonist and need one more Year Seven act. At the moment, it's all boys, so I'd really like a girl in the mix. I know it's only three days away, but I wouldn't expect you to learn anything new; just play an old favourite."

"Thanks, but I don't think—" Kiki had just begun her refusal when the lights in the room stuttered.

Mr McKenzie frowned, stepping away from his desk to stare out of the doorway, glancing up and down the corridor at the similarly stuttering lights.

Meanwhile, Kiki's eyes were fixed on the whiteboard. A minute ago, the dull PowerPoint had been frozen on an image of Saturn. Now it had silently reactivated itself, but instead of being a series of static slides, the planets had begun to *spin* on the screen. Kiki watched dumbstruck as Saturn, Mercury, Uranus and Neptune gently rotated. The vibrant red of Mars and the blinding blue of Venus were so vivid, so 3D, that Kiki winced at their brightness and beauty.

"Mr McKenzie..." she began, baffled at how a bland collection of slides could suddenly transform into something *this* cinematic.

"Sorry – yes, of course you need to get off to

your next lesson, Kiki," the teacher said, turning back to her as the image on the board reverted to the single static slide of Saturn. "But I can count on you to help me out with the performance, right? You'd be doing me a huge favour!"

"But—"

"You'll be brilliant!" Mr McKenzie insisted with a persuasive smile. "I'll see you here tomorrow lunchtime for a rehearsal. Now you'd better get going!"

Finding herself ushered out of the room, Kiki hoicked her bag up on to her shoulder and started down the corridor, her brain struggling to make sense of what she'd just seen.

"How was that even possible?" she mumbled, as she quickened her pace.

Perhaps it was a snatch of film that Mr McKenzie had bookmarked, and the electrical glitch had made his laptop display it *instead* of the PowerPoint. Kiki wasn't even sure if that was at all possible, but it was as close to an answer as she could manage.

She rounded the corner and her steps slowed as she saw that she wasn't the only one who was running late for their next lesson.

"Take it off! Take it off!" came a chant from the far end of the corridor, where a bundle of boys were in a huddle round some unlucky person. Their collective laughter had a harsh, cutting edge to it, which made Kiki hang back.

But she was close enough to recognize who they were. Harvey Wickes and his crew of Jake, Jarek and Archie were circling that weird boy Wes, who was standing in the open door of the boys' toilets. Kiki saw Harvey step forwards and roughly yank down Wes's hood, the boy's scruff of white-blond hair popping up like an exclamation mark.

Kiki hesitated. She wanted to call out Harvey and his mates for their mean jeering, but would she – should she – even dare to do it? They wouldn't pay any attention to her anyway, especially now she'd been dumped from Lola's crew. And, after the sniggering and sneering she'd faced so far this morning, her confidence had flatlined, and she didn't feel like being the target of yet *more* taunting.

And so the words that could have helped Wes stayed stuck in her throat. But as she made to sidle past them unseen, a sudden racket and roar of multiple hand dryers blasted from the toilets.

The lights inside surged, flashing off and on, the brightness spilling out of the doorway behind Wes.

"Whoa!"

"What's going on?"

"How's that happening?"

"There's no one in there!"

A jumble of voices jabbered, before Harvey and his friends began backing away, then ran off down the corridor, laughing as if that strange phenomenon hadn't spooked them at all.

Which left Wes staring back into the now quiet and still boys' toilets. As he pulled his hood back up over his messy spikes of hair, he seemed to notice Kiki hovering nearby.

Kiki hesitated, confused and awkward, not sure if she should say something about the weirdness that just happened or the meanness she'd witnessed. But before she could untangle her thoughts and decide, Wes started walking away, his too-short school trousers flapping above his ankles and worn school shoes.

What was it like to be someone like Wes? Kiki wondered. Someone who was the butt of all the jokes, casually bullied or blanked by the popular kids? Of course, she was getting a taste of that herself today...

As Kiki picked up the pace and hurried to her next class, she didn't spot the bulbs in the ceiling lights above her flare gently, spotlighting her every step.

STAR BOY: Close up, far away...

The home-time bell rang, and students jostled and spilled out of school, swapping stories of lights that had dipped and blown, whiteboards that had stuttered and stopped and photocopiers that had spontaneously spewed out reams of blank sheets.

At the same time, in the lower playground, pigeons rose into the air as the bushes parted with a rustle, and the currently invisible Star Boy stepped out. In one hand, he clutched a very visible sheet of plastic that appeared to float gently in the air.

After resetting the shield and making his pod safely unseen again, the Star Boy had come across the remnant of the Terra Firma sign that he'd spotted on the night of his crash. He'd tugged the bedraggled plastic from the grip of stubborn branches, knowing *exactly* what he would do with it.

In Observation Studies back home, his class watched images of Humans performing rituals in their homes, including spreading cloths over tables. There'd been no explanation *why* they might do that, but he thought he'd mimic the custom and spread the torn sheet of plastic over his DANGER! box.

While he was aware that tonight could be the night the rescue craft came for him, there was no harm in passing the time gathering additional Human objects of interest, and displaying them in the basement. It would make the space seem – as Humans might say – more *homely*.

But fixing the invisibility shield and finding the Terra Firma sign were just two extra wonders in this well-omened day. His Channelling had gone spectacularly well, in spite of the occasional blip. He had observed how Young Humans were taught by their Masters in a totally different format from his own, using no data lenses, no life-size projected images and no simulators. But the Star Boy had been transfixed by the art of scratching marks into paper books, making *actual written words*. It was an earthly marvel!

And, best of all, he had found out that his Human Girl specimen was named KIKI. A Master had called her that this morning as the Star Boy had stared at her through the motionless rings of Saturn. Unfortunately, he'd rather spoiled the moment by accidentally downloading moving images of planets from his data lens, but no harm had been done.

"KIKI!" He said her name aloud, thrilling at the delicious sound of it, while startling the pigeons. "KI-KI-KI!"

Now it was the Star Boy's turn to be startled. As if summoned, his Human Girl came hurrying into the lower playground, then slowed, glancing around warily at the sound of her name. While her head turned this way and that, he took the opportunity to drop the floating plastic sign to the ground, as if it was simply litter blown there.

But as soon as Kiki seemed satisfied that she was alone and sped up, the Star Boy became concerned. Was she planning to leave the Outside the way she'd arrived earlier in the day, through the shrubbery? It was odd to him that she should choose this method; from what he had studied of school-age Humans, they tended to enter and exit in a mass clump, through large, open 'gates'.

But that wasn't the important thing right now – the Star Boy was worried that Kiki might bump into his invisible pod and injure herself. And everyone from his planet knew that Humans were ridiculously fragile, and could easily damage bits of their bodies.

Then he noted with relief that Kiki was detouring *round* the tall, swaying greenery. It gave him time to take a shortcut, to rustle back through the shrubbery himself and see what it was she was looking for, an exit in the wire-mesh fence presumably. He reached it first, saw the breach, the tear in the criss-crossing metal made by his pod three night-times ago.

And now she was coming towards him, pushing along the tight gap between scratchy foliage to her left and the fence on her right. In seconds, she was by his side, her fingers trying to force the two pieces of torn metal apart.

"Come on!" Kiki raged at herself.

The Star Boy's face was inches from hers, thrillingly close. He scrutinized her face, noting her brows (furred), eyes (hair-edged), nostrils (*slightly* hairy) and her open, multi-toothed mouth (no apparent hair).

And look at the lids of her eyes, the Star Boy marvelled. *They close up and down, instead of side to side like mine ... remarkable!*

He lifted his long, fin-shaped hand, wishing he could touch the tiny spirals of dark hair that were tied high on her head and bounced as she yanked and tugged at the wire mesh.

What do those feel like? he wondered. *Soft? Squishy? Crunchy? Or—*

"AAARGH!"

A yell of distress erupted from the Human Girl, a loud surprise of a sound that *nearly* shocked the Star Boy's pulses into starting, *nearly* letting her see him in all his glowing amber glory...

"Why won't this STUPID fence come apart?" Kiki shouted.

She was clearly in difficulty. Could he help Kiki, wthout her being aware of it? Yes, he decided quickly. Wrapping his hand round the piece of wire fencing closest to him, the Star Boy synchronized with her, pulling when she did.

"Thank goodness!" Kiki groaned in relief, slipping through the newly widened space, and hurrying off down the path that edged the river.

The Star Boy watched her bound over the bridge – blazer and bag flying behind her – and realized he was experiencing a sensation he had never felt before.

Disappointment.

He was disappointed to see her go, leaving him on his own.

KIKI: Homesick for then

Ignored.

Given the side-eye.

Whispered about behind hands covering mouths.

Being 'volunteered' to perform at the school's stupid Open Evening...

As she hurried up the hill from the high street, Kiki wished she could go straight home, dive under her duvet and figure out how she could avoid school tomorrow, for the rest of this week, the rest of the term, the rest of her *life*...

But first she had to pick up Ty from Eddie's shop.

Pushing open the door of the Electrical Emporium, the jumble of noise and chaos of clutter immediately hit her. The place was like a shipwreck of junk. On either side of the room, the walls were lined with dishwashers, tumble dryers and even a vintage jukebox. Above those were rows of shelves stacked with a variety of working or semi-working or *waiting*-to-be-working lamps, toasters and assorted odds and ends.

Kiki had no idea what kind of muddled mess lurked in the back workroom of the shop, or the yard beyond where Eddie parked his clapped-out motorbike, but she imagined they were as much of a disaster zone as the front.

Kiki hopped out of the way as something careered into her feet. She looked down and after a startled second recognized Squeak in his orange plastic exercise ball. So *that's* what her brother had stuffed in his back-to-front backpack this morning.

"Ty! What are you doing to poor Squeak? You can't just take him places like a *dog*. He'll get stressed out!"

"*I'm gonna ROCK around the CLOCK...!*" Ty shouted along to a record booming out of the jukebox, blissfully oblivious to the telling-off.

As well as Ty's semi-tuneful yelling and the blast of music, the room was filled with a racket of clanking and whirring. The clanking was coming from the floor, where Ty knelt beside a spaghetti of train tracks, his lightsabre glowing but discarded nearby. The whirring noise Kiki couldn't figure out at first, till it became instantly, insistently loud.

"Hi, Kiki!" Ty yelped, suddenly spotting his big sister. "Oh – watch OUT!"

But Kiki had just spotted the incoming drone. She ducked, batting it away.

"Sorry!" Eddie called out from behind the counter, guiding the juddering drone to land beside him.

"It's OK," said Kiki, pretending it hadn't startled her. "So is that Lucas's drone? The one Ty broke on Saturday?"

"It's not MY fault it broke. I think it must've got SHOT DOWN by, like, an INVISIBLE LASER or something!" Ty said dramatically, acting out the imagined action by pointing his arms, while his sister rolled her eyes.

"Yeah, although I've not *quite* managed to fix it yet," Eddie was muttering, frowning down at the drone. "I might take it to the park to try it out in the next day or two..."

"YAY! And I can help you!" Ty said enthusiastically.

"Never mind that – Mum'll be home soon and she'll expect us to be there," Kiki pointed out. "So find your stuff, Ty, and let's—"

"Hi, guys!" Mum called out, as she entered the shop. "Got a lift back from one of the other nurses, so I'm a bit early. Thought I'd find you here!"

Ty jumped up and ran to hug her, Kiki watching as Mum snuggled him right back, as if she couldn't love him more. Suddenly a memory rushed in hard: Kiki pictured herself at Ty's age, snuggling into Dad and seeing his look of love shining down on her.

In the year Dad had been gone, these out-of-the-blue moments often caught Kiki off guard. And they always left her reeling and homesick for the way things used to be, the *old* shape of her family.

Kiki blinked, gulping the hard knot of tears away.

"Hey, Kiki!" said Mum, with Ty still bundled in a cuddle. "How did it go with Lola?"

"I … I don't really want to talk about it," mumbled Kiki, her confidence shattered after the drama of the day and her feelings suddenly too raw with remembering.

"Of course," said Mum, with an understanding nod. "We can have a catch-up later."

But Kiki was suddenly overwhelmed with a yearning, not for a catch-up with Mum – or a Mum-shaped hug – but to fill the Dad-shaped hole in her heart. Sure, there were framed photos of Dad dotted around the flat, but right now she wanted to disappear into her room and rummage in the bottom drawer of her bedside table. It was her private memory box, where she'd squirrelled away an old-fashioned CD Walkman and headphones, a blue asthma inhaler and an out-of-date bus pass with Dad's photo on. Just random stuff, junk that he hadn't taken with him, but they'd become secret treasures to Kiki.

And now snatches of Dad's favourite songs drifted through her head as she remembered the CD inside the Walkman: a home-made compilation – like a Spotify playlist – that Dad put together way before Kiki was born. Hip-hop, reggae and David Bowie tracks. Even ancient 1950s 'crooner' songs, like 'What a Wonderful World' by Louis Armstrong. He'd always launch into that on Saturday evenings, when the takeaway had just arrived and they were all settling down to watch a movie together.

That picture in Kiki's head … it made her chest ache.

There was no way she was in the right frame of mind for Mum to go on about today again.

"Tell you what, we can have a nice chat after *this* little pest goes to bed," said Mum, as Ty wriggled free, his attention focused back on the train set. "Fancy that, Kiki? Then you can tell me all about how you got on…"

With a bundle of emotions crushing together in her chest, all Kiki could manage in reply was a 'whatever' shrug. She didn't miss Mum's slight frown.

"So what mischief do we think your brother's been up to today?" Mum said cheerfully, changing the subject.

Her mum was smiling, probably expecting a knowing grin in return from Kiki. But being the butt of everyone's jokes, falling out with her friends, thinking of Dad … *everything* about today hurt.

Kiki suddenly unravelled.

"I dunno. Why don't you ask him yourself?" she snapped.

From Mum's face, she knew she'd gone too far.

"Kiki! There's no need for that tone!"

"Oh, please!" Kiki muttered not-quite-under-her-breath, somehow unable to stop herself.

"There – that sulky face you pulled! That's *just* like Lola," said Mum sharply. "You didn't used to act rudely towards me, Kiki. That attitude only started when you began hanging out with Lola and those other girls."

"Well, you'll be happy to know that they've made it *very* clear they don't want to be friends with me any more!" said Kiki, her voice raised and wobbly.

"Well, maybe I *am*!" Mum sniped back.

Ty and Eddie stared back and forth between Kiki and Mum, Ty frozen in shock, Eddie wavering, looking like he wasn't sure if he should intervene or not. Kiki felt hot and cold at the same time. She knew she'd lashed out at the wrong person, but felt hurt by Mum's terse tone.

"See you back home," mumbled Kiki to no one in particular, scooping up Squeak in his orange ball and walking out of the shop.

It would probably take a few minutes for Ty and Mum to follow, since they'd be faffing around searching for her brother's jacket and shoes and backpack. Which gave Kiki a tiny pocket of time to calm down – and quickly call Dad. She knew that hearing his hello, and the sunshine in his voice, would make everything better.

As soon as the door banged shut and she was out in the cool air, Kiki rifled in her pocket for her phone. And then she stopped dead, remembering that Dad was away for a few days with his girlfriend... With a sinking heart, Kiki put the phone back in her pocket, suddenly at a loss.

A tiny scrabble of claws caught her attention.

"Just you and me then, Squeak?" she said, lifting the plastic ball to her face and talking to the wide-eyed, whisker-twitching creature inside. "I could do with a bit of company. Even if you *are* just a furry little alien in disguise..."

Kiki's words faded as she suddenly recalled the peculiar whatever-it was she'd seen hidden in the bushes at school this morning. That shimmering, giant, egg-shaped science project, or pretend spaceship that a teacher must have made for a project.

If that had been real, she found herself musing, *what would the aliens inside have looked like?*

And then she got real. Kiki shook herself back to the present, her attention drawn by the brightly lit interior and the comforting rumble of the machines of the Busy Bubbles laundrette next door to Eddie's shop.

And there, inside, was someone familiar. Sitting on a bench was the hooded boy, Wes – but for once he wasn't wearing his ever-present Puffa jacket.

He looks sort of... Kiki paused, trying to think of the right word. And then it came to her.

Lonely.

Wes looked almost as lonely as Kiki felt.

WES: Toffees and random treasures

The lady who ran the laundrette reached into the pocket of her nylon overall and handed Wes a toffee.

"Usually just see you at the weekend, don't I?" she said.

Wes and Dad split all the chores. Dad was in charge of the housework, since he didn't go out much, and Wes did the shopping and laundry. He liked coming to the laundrette most Sundays because it gave him reading time, and if Mrs Crosby was on duty she always stopped for a chat and a sweet.

"Thanks and yep," said Wes, untwirling the toffee from its wrapper. "I spilled something on my jacket."

"Ah, well, it'll be good as new soon, Wesley!"

said Mrs Crosby, ambling off to wipe down the dryers.

The stain on his jacket was what had kicked everything off this morning with Harvey and his mates. They'd cornered Wes as he was coming out of the boys' toilets, jabbering on about the smeary curry stain he hadn't managed to clean off properly, how his trousers were too short, and asking why he wore such rubbish shoes, before Harvey had yanked his hood down.

Wes always tried not to let their stupid goading get to him. And today he barely gave the boys any thought at all; he was far too fired up by the inexplicable electrical oddness of the day. It could have been lifted from a storyline in one of his *Doctor Who* books, just like the short-but-strange storm on Friday night.

Wes suddenly felt a slight pang, wishing he had a best friend to talk over all the strangeness with. He never usually cared about being alone – he'd got used to it. He didn't see much of his mum these days. After she left, he'd stayed with her some weekends, but Wes didn't get the impression her new boyfriend was too keen on being a stepdad.

Then they'd had the twins and moved so far away that visits were difficult, turning into now-and-again phone calls instead. And, until this year, Wes had been home-schooled by his dad. But Wes felt alone in a *different* way since the two of them had moved to Fairfield and Wes started secondary school.

Most of the time he wandered between classes with nobody much noticing him, except to occasionally point and tease. Back at the flat, Dad was constantly hunched over the computer, worrying about work and money, and not always remembering regular things like registering with a doctor or talking to his son.

This 'different' sort of alone ... Wes wondered if it was what lonely felt like.

With that fleeting thought, he checked in the pocket of his school trousers for the twentieth time, making sure his few important things were safely in there. Normally, he kept them zipped up in the inside pocket of his jacket, so they were always close to his heart. They were just a few stray bits of Mum's that Wes had kept – a single star-shaped stud earring, an old silver sixpence, a shiny white shell – but they helped fill the missing-Mum void just a little bit.

"Hey, Wesley!" He suddenly heard Mrs Crosby calling over to him. "Someone's looking at you. Friend of yours, is she?"

Wes saw that Mrs Crosby was pointing towards the big glass window. He turned and immediately locked eyes with the girl who'd been dressed as Rey the other night. The one he'd seen in the lower playground this morning, when shyness made him forget how basic *speaking* worked.

But now it was the girl's turn to get it wrong. Instead of raising her free hand to wave at him, she held up a round plastic ball, which contained a hamster.

Today, Wes decided, was getting weirder and weirder...

Tuesday: How to BE a Human

STAR BOY: Into the Inside...?

The Star Boy had remained unrescued overnight.

In the darkness of the early hours, he had stood in the middle of the Outside, staring up at the star-dotted sky, and pondered. He had pondered over his lack of mechanical knowledge, and the stubbornly non-functioning location alerter and communication device. He had pondered whether or not he should disarm the invisibility shield in these quiet, hushed hours, so that a rescue craft might have more chance of finding him.

He had even pondered whether a rescue craft would come for him at all. Perhaps the planet's authorities had been scanning Earth satellites and, having seen no alarming news of an alien landing, assumed that he and the pod had blown up and disintegrated as they fell?

The Star Boy had pondered so long that the dawn light slowly grew and the world of Fairfield began to awake in a chirping of birds and the occasional buzz of distant vehicles (how he would like to see some of these charmingly simple methods of travel up close!).

Enjoying seeing the Outside come to life, the Star Boy had paused his pulses, fading his glow as the morning sun rose and the pigeons fluttered to join him in the playground.

And then it became the time of school. There'd been no appearance of the Human Boy, but the Star Boy did have the privilege of seeing Kiki the Human Girl. The creaking and twanging of the broken fence as she forced her way through had alerted him to her presence.

He'd watched her walk *round* the shrubbery rather than wriggle *through* it, so there was no risk of her bumping into the unseen pod. And yet the Star Boy did wonder at the way she had peered into the foliage... What was she expecting to see? *Had* she spotted a glimpse of the pod yesterday morning after all? But at the sound of what he now understood to be a bell, he saw Kiki smile and shake her head – as if realizing she'd been foolish, or mistaken, he thought.

As she'd hurried off to begin her day's learning, the Star Boy had returned to the basement and the DANGER! box to practise his Channelling. He was pleased to note that his skills were becoming more refined: he'd zipped round the school's electrical pathways with much less disruption than the previous day. He trailed his two specimens with greater ease, while they moved and weaved round the various buildings. The only thing that had gone wrong was fusing all the lights in a room where he watched Human Masters gather and eat biscuits.

As the middle of the day came – a short period when all the Humans refuelled – the Star Boy took a welcome break himself. He now stood, arms outstretched, in the middle of the playground, absorbing the glow of the sun on his invisible skin. In doing so, his left arm had accidentally become a perch for his pigeon friend, but he didn't mind. He welcomed the chance to study it close up, and welcomed the company too.

"As it is lunching-time, do you think the Human

Boy will come to sit on the steps again?" the Star Boy turned and asked the pigeon, testing out his spoken English on the creature, trying to remember vocabulary without double-checking it on his data lens.

He didn't have to hope for long, because *here* came his Human now, clutching his block of paper in one hand. In the other, he held a triangular plastic package and the fruit known as a banana.

"You'd better go," the Star Boy urged the bird, encouraging it to *thwack-thwack-THWACK* away with a shake of his shoulder. It might be confusing for the Human Boy to see a bird sitting in mid-air.

"Hey, Wes!" came a shout from behind the Boy. "I wouldn't have your lunch outside today!"

"Oh, uh, OK, Mr Shah," the Boy muttered and blink-blinked, sounding confused.

So the man who was often busy by the bins was known as Mr Shah. And this Mr Shah had *just* spoken the name of his specimen: Wes! Now the Star Boy knew the names of *both* his specimens: WES and KIKI.

"You'd better get yourself indoors," the Human called Mr Shah continued. "It's going to tip down any second."

- *tip down* =

The Star Boy didn't get a chance to search his data; he tilted his head to look upwards at the rapidly incoming bank of clouds and water sprayed down on him from the sky.

- *tip down = rain heavily*

Now all the pigeons rose from the ground as one, spinning and wheeling off in search of shelter. But the Star Boy loved everything about the tippy-tapping sensation on his skin, and was perfectly happy to stay in the Outside and experience it.

Of course, there was something *else* he could do, the Star Boy suddenly realized, as he watched Wes walk away. He was getting stronger, not having to recharge so quickly. So instead of Channelling this afternoon, perhaps he could test exactly how long he could pause his pulses for.

Holding his arms wide to catch the rain instead of the sun, he began to follow Wes into the other busier, noisier Outside.

Perhaps he might end up on the *Inside* too...

WES: Rudely interrupted

Soaked from the sudden shower of rain, steam rose from Wes's sopping-wet jacket, a genie-like spiral of it twirling from the top of his hood.

He didn't notice. He was too lost in his book, standing in the reading nook he'd just made for himself in the busy, noise-fuelled corridor. Behind him, the heat from the radiator rose up to warm his damp back, and the vending machine he was leaning his shoulder up against gave out a soothing hum.

Until...

"Whoa – what's this? A comic?" Harvey Wilkes bellowed.

Wes paused for a second, wondering if he should point out that *Star Trek: None But the Brave* was a graphic novel and not a comic. And that anyway comics were very cool, actually.

But he knew he'd just be wasting his time, especially since Harvey had an audience. His three football teammates were hovering close by, as well as the perfect and perfectly awful Lola whatshername that the tall, skinny girl from the party usually hung out with. But the girl-who-was-Rey wasn't with Lola today; it was just the other two, slouching and posing by Lola's side.

"Yep, it's a comic," Wes replied flatly. He looked back down at the excellent illustrations on the page of his damp-edged book.

"Good, is it?" Harvey changed tack, flicking repeatedly at the cover with his finger.

"Yep," said Wes, lifting the book up out of flicking range.

"Yeah, but is it? Is it?" Harvey chattered, leaning in close and blinking his eyes, copycatting Wes's tic.

Wes blinked back blankly, hearing the hoots of laughter that buoyed up Harvey's bullying.

"Everything all right here?" a voice suddenly called out.

Wes recognized the man weaving through the crush of students towards them as Mr McKenzie, one of the music teachers.

"Absolutely, sir!" Harvey answered with a cheeky grin.

"Good to hear!" said Mr McKenzie, shooting a pointed look at Harvey. "So how about you finish up what you're doing here, and you and your mates move on?"

"Yes, sir. Course, sir," Harvey replied with mock politeness, as he scanned the cold drink choices.

Mr McKenzie turned back to Wes with a genuine smile. "Got caught in that downpour, did you? Come with me and let's get that jacket dried off before afternoon classes."

"*Teacher's pet...*"

The words were hissed by Harvey as he squatted down to put his hand inside the metal flap, ready to catch the drink he'd selected.

But, with a sudden rumble, the vending machine malfunctioned spectacularly, dropping every can from every row. The drawer flap was jammed on top of Harvey's hand, trapping it inside, where it was pummelled by can after cold, hard can.

"Ow! Help! Make it stop!" Harvey whined, as his mates and Lola and co burst out laughing.

Wes kept his face neutral, but whispered a barely there, "YESSSS!" to himself.

KIKI: When pulses unpause

"Hey, Kiki, good to see you!" said Mr McKenzie in his usual infectiously enthusiastic way.

Kiki put on a fake smile as the classroom door slapped shut behind her. She didn't particularly want to be here, but she couldn't think of anywhere else to go. Every corner of the school that she turned, it was the same as yesterday, the photo-sharing and shaming rumbling on. She could tell by the staring, sniggering and back-turning. How was it possible to feel so noticed but ignored at the same time...?

"Here you go!" said Mr McKenzie, reaching for one of the multicoloured ukuleles hanging from hooks on the music-room wall.

"Um, thanks..." said Kiki, reluctantly taking the bright red uke from him, though the texture of the neck in her hand *did* feel good.

"So what have you decided to perform at the concert?" asked Mr McKenzie.

"Um, I thought maybe 'What a Wonderful World...'"

"By Louis Armstrong? Good choice! That's a real classic. Parents will *love* that," said Mr McKenzie, ushering Kiki over to a semicircle of blue plastic chairs. All of them were empty – except for one.

Wes blink-blinked at Kiki, a pair of hand drums wedged between his knees. She noticed his Puffa jacket steaming gently on the radiator behind him. The same as when she spotted him in the laundrette the day before, he looked strangely naked without it on.

"Don't know if you two know each other...?" said Mr McKenzie, only to be met with awkward, silent shrugs on both sides, which hardly answered his question. "Kiki, this is Wes. Wes, this is Kiki. Now, hey – *here's* a thought! How about you two perform *together* at the Open Evening? Wes can accompany you, Kiki. I've just been listening to him play – he's a natural on the bongos!"

Kiki was too stunned to stutter out a reply.

Wes just looked a bit startled.

"Do you know 'What a Wonderful World', Wes?" asked Mr McKenzie, taking his buzzing phone out of his jacket pocket.

"I think so, but I'm not too—"

"Good, good, I'm sure you'll pick it up!" Mr McKenzie said distractedly, staring at the screen of his mobile. "Sorry – Mrs Evans wants to see me about the timings for the Open Evening. Back in a few minutes. Why don't you two run through the song together and I'll hear how it's sounding shortly?"

With that, the door clunked shut, leaving Kiki and Wes languishing in an uncomfortable silence.

Trumm-trummmm...

"Sorry," mumbled Wes, lifting his fingers off the drums. "Can't help doing that."

"It's OK," Kiki muttered, sinking down on to the nearest chair, since she couldn't think what else to do.

Resting the ukulele on her lap, she glanced over at Wes and noticed that he was as wet as his jacket. His spiky hair stuck limply to his forehead.

"Is it raining or did you just take a shower?" she

asked, managing a weak joke.

Wes seemed to like the joke, however weak it was, and smiled shyly back at her.

"Yeah, it started raining pretty hard out there..."

As Wes spoke, he turned to glance out of the window – where a pigeon sat on the sill outside, shaking raindrops off its wings.

His smile spread to a grin and he thrummed his fingers on the drums. "Y'know, I saw this totally weird thing in the lower playground about ten minutes ago. A pigeon was sitting in mid-air. Not flying or hovering, just sitting. Like it was perched on an invisible branch or something!"

Kiki stared at him, thinking of the oddness *she'd* seen.

"If it makes you feel any better, yesterday morning I thought I saw something weird in the lower playground too. Just before we, um, ran into each other."

"Oh yeah? What sort of something?" Wes asked, perking up and shaking off his shyness.

Kiki frowned. "This is going to sound nuts, but when I was pushing my way through the bushes I saw this huge, shimmering *blob* thing."

She paused – as did Wes – at the sound of a sudden soft whine. But it stopped almost as soon as it started, so she carried on.

"But when I went to look for it this morning, it was gone. It was probably just some giant novelty balloon. I suppose Mr Shah dragged it out of the bushes and chucked it in the bins."

"Maybe," Wes agreed.

Kiki felt suddenly silly for imagining the giant balloon-blob-thing was anything more than just that. And that she'd gone nosying around in the bushes like a complete fool this morning.

"So you're friends with that Lola?" said Wes, in the small gap in their conversation.

By the way he said 'that Lola', Kiki could tell Wes didn't think much of her. Any other time, Kiki would have dived right in to defend Lola, out of loyalty. But after the way things had been the last few days, she wasn't sure that she wanted to.

"Sort of," Kiki answered vaguely, as she began to gently strum a few chords. "So what made you want to play at the Open Evening?"

She saw Wes hesitate, obviously noting the change of subject. Luckily, he just went with it.

"I didn't. All that happened was Mr McKenzie said I should come and dry my jacket in here," said Wes, his fingers softly padding out a rhythm to match what Kiki was playing. "Maybe he thought I needed rescuing or something."

"Rescuing?" Kiki repeated.

"Someone was trying to give me a hard time," said Wes, giving another little shrug.

"Let me guess – Harvey Wilkes again?" Kiki asked, feeling cross on Wes's behalf.

"Again?" Wes said, sounding confused.

Kiki's fingers stalled a little and she shuffled in her seat. This was going to sound like she'd been spying on him.

"I saw him and his mates hassling you in the corridor yesterday morning," she said, keeping her eyes on her fingers as she strummed, rather than look Wes in the eye.

"Yeah ... guess it's starting to become a habit," said Wes, trying to joke it away.

"*Achooo!*"

The funny little sound made Kiki glance up. Who would have guessed Wes sneezed like a kitten?

"Bless you!" she said automatically.

But the stunned expression on Wes's face told her straight away that he wasn't the one doing the sneezing.

"Achooo!"

It was the other person in the semicircle of blue plastic chairs. The one with sparks flying out of its mouth when it sneezed.

The creature sitting in between them, glowing vivid amber.

WES: Saying hello to the lost boy

Two chairs screeched in unison as Wes and Kiki jumped to their feet.

"That ... *that* wasn't there! And now it is!" Wes babbled, clutching the drums tightly to his chest.

"What is it?" Kiki said, ukulele dangling uselessly by her side. "Is it some kind of trick?"

Both of them instantly squinted round the room in a panic, desperately looking for a projector, a practical-joking student, an answer.

"*Achooo!*"

At the pathetic, ordinary sort of noise, Wes turned back to look at the creature. At first glance, he couldn't see any obvious joins in the costume, any zips or Velcro, any holes for eyes, any *possible* way it could glow the way it was glowing.

At second glance, he noted that it was vaguely human in shape and size, but completely smooth and shiny. It was impossible to tell where its skin or clothing or whatever started and ended.

"Is it all right?" Wes whispered to Kiki.

"I don't know!" she answered in a panic.

"*Uh, uh, uh...*"

Wes froze, uncertain what the creature was about to say or do next. But the sound it was making wasn't a stream of words: it was fast and juddering breaths, its mouth a tiny dark dot of a startled 'oh!', nostrils small slits, currently fluttering like a goldfish out of water. And those too-huge black eyes. They were wide, so wide, with eyelids that rapidly flipped open and shut, from side to freaky side.

"Are you OK? Do you need help?" Wes asked the being.

"*Uh, uh, uh...*" The creature panted some more, as if it had been holding its breath and was now gulping down oxygen as fast as it could.

"Do you ... do you have asthma, maybe?" suggested Wes.

He saw Kiki turn and stare disbelievingly at him.

"'Do you have *asthma*?'" she repeated incredulously.

"*Really*, Wes? We're in a room with … with something that's just materialized out of thin air and *that's* the question you ask?"

Wes was sure that Kiki had been about to say 'alien', but then stopped herself, as if she couldn't quite believe that's what they were actually sharing a classroom with. He supposed Kiki was clinging on to the hope that there *had* to be another explanation for whatever it was. Wes was hoping there wasn't.

"It's just that its breathing sounds kind of *bad*," Wes replied, putting his drums down on the floor with trembling hands. "Like when *my* asthma's playing up. Which it kind of is right now. I've got my pump…"

While Wes grabbed his jacket from the radiator and started patting the pockets, he studied the creature, noticing tiny upward movements *just* visible in its left eye, like the scrolling of a screen on a mobile phone.

"EEEE-KTT-KTT-CRRREEEEEE-AAAAG!" it squawked and screeched suddenly.

Wes jerked in surprise, while Kiki took another step back, clunking the ukulele against a chair. The loud *TWANNNGGG!* of it made the creature jerk.

It made another noise. This time it was a noise which both Wes and Kiki understood.

"Sorry. Sorry for alarm. I forgot to translate from my language," it said stiltedly, but in recognizable English.

Wes let his jacket drop, forgetting to search for his inhaler now that the glowing amber entity had become talkative.

"So what was it that you were trying to ... to *communicate* to us just now?" Wes asked, picking his words carefully.

Excitement began to surge in his chest. Surely now was the time he and Kiki would find out if this was an incredibly sophisticated practical joke ("Ha! Got you!"), or an incredibly sophisticated *actual* alien ("I've come to take you to my planet!").

"I am trying to *communicate* to you," it began, copying Wes's tone of voice, "that I am not having 'asthma'."

Out of the corner of his eye, Wes saw Kiki shake her head a little, as if she was slightly stunned that they were all chatting casually about asthma instead of finding out what on earth was going on.

But Wes's gaze was now drawn to the creature's

hands. Was it wearing glossy mittens of some sort? he wondered. Wes noted a thumb on each hand, but couldn't make out any fingers, just a strangely long, elegant fin shape where you'd expect to see them.

"What ARE you?" he heard Kiki say bluntly, finding her voice at last.

The creature stared at her, its eyes doing the unsettling sideways blink.

"I am a Star Boy," it replied matter-of-factly.

A *piece of the puzzle was solved*, thought Wes. At least they knew it was a *male* something.

"A Star Boy ... as in an actual boy from *space*?" Wes asked in wonder.

"Yes, correct," replied the alien, staring back at Wes with an equally awestruck expression.

"I knew it!" said Wes, almost jumping up and down on the spot. "The storm on Friday – was that when you arrived? I was *sure* I saw something dropping from the clouds!"

"Yes, that is correct. My pod was damaged four night-times ago," the Star Boy answered Wes's question. "I fell to Earth. I landed here in *terra firma*."

Wes didn't understand what the alien meant by *terra firma*, but before he could ask him more, Kiki jumped in.

"I was on the riverside path during the storm!" she said.

That must have been soon after he'd seen Kiki leave Lola's house, Wes realized.

"Yes, I saw you," the alien answered Kiki. "I had just exited my damaged pod. I was assessing where I was. I watched you through the wire wall called fencing. You waved around a torch device."

"My brother's lightsabre," Kiki muttered. "And wait a minute; your spaceship ... it's in the big clump of bushes in the lower playground, isn't it? I saw it! Didn't I just say that to you, Wes?"

Wes nodded energetically.

"Only it's not there any more!" said Kiki, turning back to the alien.

"It *is* still there," the Star Boy assured her. "But the invisibility shield is now activated."

Wes and Kiki glanced at each other, both their heads whirling as it dawned on them that what they were looking at was no illusion: this 'Star Boy' really, truly was an alien.

Dozens of questions were rattling and racing round Wes's head, but he asked the first that came out of his mouth.

"I know you crashed, but why did you come here in the first place? What's so special about Fairfield?"

"*Special...?*" the Star Boy repeated Wes's question, sounding genuinely confused. "There is nothing *special* about Fairfield. It is simply part of our education to come to a randomly appointed area of Earth and observe."

"Like a geography field trip?" asked Wes.

The Star Boy hesitated before answering, scrolling in the corner of one eye once again.

"Yes, that is correct. Like a geography field trip," he confirmed. "The journeying to Earth and back also tests our piloting and orienteering skills. But setting storms was not on our educational itinerary, and is expressly against the rules. I apologize for the irresponsible actions of the Others."

"The others? Other Star Boys?" Wes practically gasped.

"Yes, that is correct," said the alien. "They know they must not shoot bolts while in the Earth's atmosphere, as the electrical charges are likely to cause sudden, dramatic weather events. They did it once before and our Master berated us, ordering us to undertake the observation again, and behave more appropriately. But the Others ... forgot. They caused another storm and I was accidentally shot down."

Wes stared at Kiki, and Kiki stared at Wes. Both the unpredicted storms seemed – bizarrely – to make a whole lot more sense now.

"My brother Ty said he saw spaceships during last month's storm. He told the TV reporter about it the next day," Kiki told them both. "I thought he was lying. He lies all the time about everything. But he was telling the *truth* for once!"

"Hold on; that was your brother?" Wes said in surprise. "I saw him when I was being interviewed!"

"TV is *television*. I know this," the Star Boy butted in. "We stream it from your satellites so that we may learn about you."

Wes stared hard at the alien, wondering what exactly his 'people' might choose to watch. The news? Wildlife documentaries? Reality shows? Sci-fi movies? And then he thought of a more important, obvious question to ask.

"Where are you from? I mean, what's the name of your planet?"

The Star Boy made the tiniest of sounds in reply, like a small sigh.

"Can you translate that into English?" Kiki asked.

The alien blinked thoughtfully and sideways for a moment.

"No," he announced. "Not in words. But it is like *this...*"

The creature lifted a hand, making a small movement in the air with its 'thumb', as if it was dotting an 'i'.

"OK..." said Wes with a frown. The name of the Star Boy's planet was surprisingly unimpressive.

"So apart from coming here from –"

Wes watched Kiki awkwardly dab a dot in the air with her finger as she talked.

"– and mucking around, causing storms, you're not here to *do* anything to the planet or us?"

"No. Earth is not of much interest to my planet. It is not advanced enough," the Star Boy stated.

"You mean it's a bit too *boring* for you?" Wes checked.

"Definitely. Very boring to my people," the

Star Boy confirmed. "But not to me. I like to study Earth and its inhabitants. So, while I am stranded, I decided it should be a learning opportunity. I chose two Human specimens to study – Wes and Kiki. I have been observing you closely for the last two days."

"You know our *names*?" said Wes, sounding delighted.

"*How* exactly have you been observing us?" Kiki demanded, her question overlapping Wes's.

"I have watched you on the Outside, near to the dense shrubbery that conceals my pod. I first watched Wes through the glass of the down-below room I am sheltering in."

"The basement? You were watching me when I was sitting on the steps?" Wes said incredulously.

"Yes, that is correct. And I have noted that Kiki likes to use an unusual entrance and exit to the school, not used by others. Why is this, Kiki? I wish to understand."

Kiki glanced from the Star Boy to Wes, who seemed to be keen to hear the answer to that too.

"I... I just wasn't in the mood to use the main entrance, that's all," she said.

"And so you scrabbled through a hole in the fence, and all the bushes?" Wes asked her, remembering how odd it had seemed at the time.

Kiki blushed and looked slightly frazzled.

"I just wanted to avoid some people, OK?" she answered tetchily, and Wes wondered if she meant Lola and the other girls that Kiki normally hung out with. "But that's hardly important right now, is it?"

Kiki quickly turned and faced the alien again. "What I want to know is how we could be watched and not know it? Is it because you can turn yourself invisible whenever you want?"

"Yes, invisibility is a skill that I am gaining confidence in," the Star Boy said with a nod. "And I have been practising another, which allows me to watch you on the Inside."

Wes joined Kiki in staring wordlessly at the Star Boy, till he understood that neither of them had a clue what he meant.

"I can observe you remotely when you are inside these buildings," the Star Boy explained. "I have trained my senses to course through the school's electrical circuits and equipment. It is called Channelling."

His expressive, fin-like hands moved in an excited orange blur as he tried to explain the skill he was so thrilled to have learned.

Kiki frowned. "Yesterday morning ... I saw all these planets spinning on the whiteboard behind our teacher's head," she said. "Did you cause that? Was it because you were watching me?"

"Yes, that is correct. It was my first experience of Channelling. Yesterday morning," he said with emphasis, copying Kiki's words, "I was careless and caused some electrical irregularities. My skills are much improved and more reliable *this* day."

"Hey, were you 'channelled' into the vending machine just now, when Harvey's hand got trapped?" asked Wes, a grin twitching at the corner of his mouth.

"What's this?" said Kiki, her ears pricking up.

"No, that is not correct. I was not Channelling – I was there, standing very close to you," the Star Boy answered Wes. "Channelling is very informative, but this day I wanted to experience the Inside properly. So I became unseen and followed you into the building from the Outside."

"How do you become 'unseen'?" asked Wes.

"I pause my pulses," said the Star Boy. "Humans cannot pause their pulses too long, I think."

"Not too long, no," said Kiki. "Or they become a bit dead..."

"Ah, I see," the Star Boy replied with an earnest nod.

"So what happened with the drinks cans?" Wes asked.

"It was an accidental occurrence. I was observing the other Human Boy's behaviour and found it confusing and conflicting. It made me lose control and surge. I am sorry if I damaged the hand of the boy reaching inside."

"I wouldn't be too sorry about that," muttered Kiki.

"But then, after that, you followed me in here?" Wes quizzed the alien some more.

"Yes, that is correct. I planned to remain unseen, but I became aware of a shaking sensation in my head and small explosions burst out of me here," said the Star Boy, pointing to the nostril-like slits in the middle of his face. "I could not control my pulses and so became visible to you."

"You sneezed!" Kiki explained. "Probably cos

you've come in from the rain to this warm room."

The Star Boy tilted his head, the scrolling speeding up in his liquid-black eye.

"What IS that?" asked Wes, stepping closer.

"My data lens. I am researching 'sneezed'. We have no experience of this on my planet. I now understand the phenomenon."

"So it's like having a miniature computer in your eye?" Wes asked him.

"Yes," said the Star Boy, widening his eye side to side so Wes could see the lens better.

"Wow!" muttered Wes.

"Wow!" the alien repeated in something that sounded like delight.

Kiki's frowning face caught Wes's attention. The fact was an alien had appeared in the music room at Riverside Academy, Fairfield. And Wes guessed she wanted to know when it might *dis*appear.

"What happens now?" she asked. "Are you stuck here forever?"

"No. A rescue craft will find me."

"You mean *more* aliens are coming?" murmured Wes.

"Yes, that is correct. Rescue craft have a crew

of very experienced Elders, but you will not see them. They will come in the quiet of a night-time. *This* night-time perhaps."

Wes let go of the breath he didn't know he'd been holding as another thought brought him back down to Earth. Something was likely to happen a *lot* sooner than an alien rescue mission tonight. Something like his discovery by a laid-back but probably still easily shockable music teacher.

"Mr McKenzie will be here any minute," he announced hurriedly. "Things could get complicated if he sees you. Can you ... *invisibilize* yourself again?"

"Yes."

The Star Boy held himself still, faded a little, then glowed amber as brightly as ever.

"No I cannot," he contradicted himself. "I have energy left but not sufficient to become unseen. To do that I need to get back to my shelter and recharge at the DANGER! box."

"You need to get back to the basement?" asked Wes.

"Yes, that is correct," the Star Boy said with a very certain nod.

"OK, but how are you going to do that?" asked Kiki. "It's lunchtime and it's raining. The hallways will be rammed with students."

"We'll have to hide him somewhere," said Wes, turning to Kiki. "Till he can sneak back at the end of the day or something..."

"Hide him? Us?!" Kiki said in surprise. "How? Where?"

"Maybe I do not need to hide?" The Star Boy calmly interrupted her panic.

His meaning became obvious as the room grew dimmer, the luminous amber of his skin fading.

"What are you doing?" asked Wes, looking the alien up and down as his colouring mutated from rich, radiant honey tones to something softer, duller and more like skin.

"I am attempting Morphing. I have studied it but not practised it before. Is it working?"

"Yeah..." murmured Wes, as he stared at the boy, who suddenly appeared passably human, complete with the usual number of fingers. A human who looked weirdly familiar, as if he'd melded himself into a version of a person based on both the people he was currently sharing a space with.

His skin was a shade lighter than Kiki's, a shade darker than Wes's. His hair was as chocolate-coloured as Kiki's, as short and spiky as Wes's. His all-black eyes now had storm-grey irises, as if the brown of Kiki's eyes and the blue of Wes's had been swirled together. He was as tall and skinny as Kiki, as male as Wes.

And that *last* issue was the problem.

"Wes..." Kiki muttered, nudging him sharply with her elbow.

"Uh-oh," Wes muttered.

Mr McKenzie might not have the heart-stopping surprise of walking in on an alien in his classroom, but Wes was pretty certain he'd have a problem with finding a completely naked boy in there.

KIKI: Hiding in plain sight

Kiki stared up and down the busy corridor. She was standing guard, ready to hammer out a warning on the classroom door if she spotted Mr McKenzie.

But there was no need. She stumbled backwards as Wes yanked the door open.

"Ta-dah!" he called out, waving Kiki back inside the classroom.

"Ta-dah!" the Star Boy repeated, his face lit up with happiness.

Kiki felt her shoulders relax. She closed the door and nodded her approval. In the last few minutes, Wes had shown himself to be a startlingly good problem-solver, liar and thief.

The problem-solving involved dressing the boy-shaped alien in school uniform, so he could blend in for the next few hours. The lying and thieving involved Wes crossing the hall to the school office, where he told Mrs Murphy, the receptionist, that he'd lost his PE shorts and could he please look for them in the lost-property cupboard. Wes had returned to the music classroom five minutes later with an impressive bundle of clothes – including school shoes hidden under his still-damp jacket. The one thing Kiki wasn't so sure of was Wes's styling.

"Really?" she said, pointing to the navy padded jacket with the hood tied too tightly round the Star Boy's eager face.

The trousers were the right length at least, though the clumpy black shoes looked a couple of sizes too big.

"It's the best I could do," said Wes. "I didn't have a lot of time..."

"Yeah, but he doesn't have to be your lookalike," said Kiki, walking over to the much-taller-than-Wes Star Boy and pulling the hood down. "Though I guess he looks like he could fit in around here for a while."

The next part of Wes's plan was to wander about with the disguised Star Boy till the end-of-lunchtime bell rang, then bundle him into the boys' toilets, where the alien would hide till Wes and Kiki came to collect him at the end of the school day and 'casually' walk him to the lower playground and the safety of his basement.

"You're hiding in plain sight – that's the name for it," said Wes.

"Hiding in plain sight," the Star Boy repeated, his data lens scrolling fast.

"Don't do that!" Kiki snapped at him.

The Star Boy flinched, blinking madly, and Kiki instantly felt bad. "Sorry, but if you do that scrolling thing when we're outside in the corridor you'll just draw attention to yourself."

"Yes, I understand that," the Star Boy said with a nod.

"But don't do that either!" she added, as he did his unnerving side-to-side blink.

The Star Boy quickly squirmed his eyes back to a regulation human shape, and nodded. "Sorry. Thank you for assisting me."

"You're welcome," Kiki answered, suddenly realizing quite how tricky it was going to be to pass this creature off as an actual human. "So we need to get out of here before Mr McKenzie comes back and starts asking awkward ques—"

"Apologies!" said Mr McKenzie, blustering back into the classroom. "Couldn't get Mrs Evans to shut up. Though I probably shouldn't say that about the head teacher. Ha!"

Kiki and Wes exchanged glances and tried very quickly and very hard to look normal, as if this was just a regular student standing between them, and not an unexpected alien in disguise.

"Oh, hello... Have you two recruited someone *else* for your band?" Mr McKenzie asked cheerfully, looking the Star Boy up and down.

"Er, no," Kiki blurted out, sounding as flustered as she felt.

"He's new!" said Wes. "And he's sort of lost..."

"Lost? Well, I'm sure you'll soon find your way around!" Mr McKenzie said with a jovial smile. "So where have you come from?"

"A very, very long way," said the Star Boy, turning round to point out of the window.

"Birmingham," Kiki jumped in, thinking of Dad's newly adopted hometown.

"Well, I'm Mr McKenzie, head of Music.

And your name is?"

"I am a Star Boy."

"Stan Boyd," Wes said quickly. "His name is Stan Boyd, sir."

"And what form are you—"

"Sorry, we have to go now," Kiki said quickly, hoisting her backpack up on to her shoulder.

"Excuse me, but I need to recharge," said the Star Boy.

"He means he hasn't had lunch yet – we're taking him to the dining hall. I got told to mentor him," Wes added, nudging the Star Boy to follow Kiki towards the door.

"Oh right – well, Kiki and Wes, you can rehearse in here for the next couple of lunchtimes," Mr McKenzie called after them. "So see you tomorrow, same time, same place!"

"Cool!" Kiki called back over her shoulder.

She had no idea how anything could be cool ever again. While other students were picking tomatoes out of their sandwiches and moaning about homework, she'd been just a few classrooms away, making small talk with an alien.

"What is a 'stanboid', please?" asked the Star

Boy, as they passed by the office, Wes giving Mrs Murphy a wave at the reception window. The alien waved too.

"Stan Boyd," Wes muttered, yanking the Star Boy's arm down, since he was holding it so high it looked as if he was asking Mrs Murphy permission to ask a question. "It's a human-sounding name. It's all I could come up with when Mr McKenzie asked who you were."

"Stan ... Boyd..." the Star Boy repeated experimentally. "Stan ... Boyd... I have never had an individual name before."

"What do your family and friends call you?" asked Kiki, pushing the entrance-hall door open and heading out into the open air, where the rain had stopped, and weak sunshine was steaming the dampness away.

There was no reply. Kiki turned to see that the Star Boy wasn't walking with them any more. Instead, he'd stopped dead and was staring round at the other students in the main playground like a Victorian Antarctic explorer coming across a colony of penguins for the first time.

"Hello! I am a HUMAN and I am called STAN

BOYD!" he suddenly called out.

"Nope! Don't do that!" Kiki warned him quickly, as a few students nearby turned to look – and laugh. "Just copy whatever we do and don't do anything to attract attention."

"Kiki, Wes – what does THIS face represent?" the Star Boy chattered on, as he fell in beside them.

Confused, Kiki looked and saw that his wide-eyed smile of wonder at the world of school had now been replaced by a cartoonish scowl.

"Why are you doing that?" she asked.

"I am replicating this expression from *them*," he said, lifting his whole arm again to point at three girls slouching on a bench close by.

"He's talking about your friends," Wes mumbled to Kiki.

Kiki glanced at where Stan was pointing and immediately wished she hadn't. Her former best friends, Lola, Zainab and Saffron, were all staring dead-eyed at them.

"They're not my friends. Not any more," she muttered.

Before Kiki could grab the Star Boy's arm, Lola held up her mobile, snapping a photo that would no doubt be posted with some snarky message. It was one of Lola's favourite pastimes – Kiki should know: she'd sat beside her plenty of times and giggled when she posted similar stuff.

"But please explain," Stan carried on regardless. "What do their facial expressions signify?"

"It's called sneering," Wes informed the Star Boy.

"What is the meaning behind 'sneering'?" he asked.

"To be horrible," said Kiki, pulling Stan away by the sleeve of his jacket.

"Do they enjoy being 'horrible'?" asked Stan.

"Yep, they do," replied Kiki, tight-lipped.

She could feel Wes's eyes on her, probably wondering what the story was with her and Lola. This wasn't the time to go into it. It probably never would be; she didn't exactly know Wes well.

"Human interaction ... there is so much to learn about it," said the Star Boy. "You will help me understand everything – yes?"

"Hardly!" said Kiki, leading the boys off in a circuit of the main playground that was as far away from her old friends as possible. "You might get rescued tonight, so there's not exactly time to learn 'everything'!"

"Actually, that's what me and, er, Stan were talking about when he was getting dressed," said Wes, looking a bit sheepish. "We were thinking that maybe the three of us could hang out after school, and we could show him some stuff."

"What sort of 'stuff'?" Kiki asked, frowning.

"There is ONE earthly marvel I wish to experience!" said the Star Boy, his eyes shining with excitement. "Is it possible that I can travel in a Human vehicle?"

Kiki stared at Stan. Here was an alien who flew spaceships at unimaginable speeds over unimaginable distances. How could anything in Fairfield compare with that?

"We *could* catch a number thirty-two on the high street after school...?" suggested Wes.

"A 'number thirty-two'! What is that? It sounds very, very interesting!" the Star Boy gushed.

"Stan," said Kiki, putting a hand on his shoulder. "Trust me, it's not."

WES: Earthly marvels (part 1)

Wes drummed his fingers on his lap, tapped his foot on the floor and couldn't stop grinning.

This was THE most astounding thing that had ever happened to him in his entire, not-very-astounding life so far. He was sitting at the front of the top deck on a number 32 bus on the Fairfield bypass NEXT TO AN ALIEN.

An alien in rumpled school uniform and a pair of orange plastic sunglasses, which Kiki had dug out of the dusty side pocket of her backpack. They looked mildly ridiculous for a drizzly Tuesday afternoon in October, but were the perfect cover for the Star Boy to scroll his data lens to his heart's content.

"I am STAN. Hello, I AM Stan. My *name* is Stan..." He quietly recited his alternative name in alternative ways, as if the taste of it was as sweet as toffee in his mouth.

He was perched bolt upright on the edge of the seat, his head turning this way and that to soak up the views outside the large window: views of hills, farms and woods on one side of the busy dual carriageway, hospital, housing estates and retail parks on the other.

Wes blink-blinked at him, trying to clear his mind, trying to figure out where to start with the big questions about Stan's life, his planet, his powers. But first he needed to do a quick something to help him blend in.

"Here," said Wes, leaning forward and straightening up the sunglasses, positioning the curved end of the arms over rather than inside Stan's ears.

"You remind me of my little brother right now," Kiki said to Stan from the seat across the aisle. "He always likes to sit up here when we go on the bus."

Kiki was grinning, Wes noticed, but she still looked a bit on edge, as if the other passengers might realize any second now that a being from another planet was in their midst and totally freak out. But the only other passenger was a snoozing old man, who might or might not have missed his stop by now.

"A brother – that is a member of the same family unit," Stan stated, sounding pleased with himself. "Kiki, you say he is little. You mean he is little like this?"

Stan raised his hand to about toddler height from the floor.

"Or like this?"

Stan held his fingers close, about a peanut size apart.

"Um, definitely nearer the first guess," she answered, laughing out loud for the first time in days. "Maybe a bit taller."

"You don't have a brother then, Stan? Or a sister?" Wes asked, spotting a chance to find out more about the Earth tourist.

"We do not live in family units of Mother, Father, children."

"To be fair, we don't necessarily, either," said Kiki. "There are lots of different ways to be a family or looked after. I live with my mum and brother."

"I live with my dad," Wes chipped in. "So who

DO you live with, Stan?"

"I live with the Others at the Education Zone, since always."

"Like a boarding school?" asked Wes, and got a nod in reply, once the split-second scrolling was over. "What about your parents?"

"Yes, there were biological parentings in my beginning. But it is not expected to ever know each other."

"Your planet sounds very *different*..." said Wes, wondering which of the human-imagined planets and peoples he'd read about *most* matched Stan's world.

"It is similar in many ways. Young ones learn and older ones work," said Stan. "There is Inside and there is Outside. But where I come from, it all looks the same. All very bright, always. All very warm, always, with electric currents and hot winds that blow. We are not powered by food, like you, but by energy. And so there are no plants of any kind. Or animals."

"So ... not at ALL similar to Earth then," Kiki checked, scrunching her nose up.

"No. Perhaps not," Stan replied thoughtfully, scrunching his own nose up to match Kiki's.

"It's weird to think you might be back there soon," Wes pointed out, remembering that the rescue party could come for Stan tonight. "So is there anything else you'd like to see or do?"

Stan's response to the question took him by surprise.

"AAAAA-EEEEEEE!"

The ear-piercing, very un-human squeal made Wes gasp, his chest tightening.

"Shh!" Kiki hissed.

"What is it? What's wrong?" asked Wes.

"Nothing is wrong – it is right!" Stan replied, pointing out of the window. "I know what I want to see next. It is there! It is a good omen, like the first night I came to Earth!"

Wes turned to see what had got his new friend so excited.

It was a long, concrete building, one of several clustered together in the nearby retail park. On its flat roof glowed a giant, gaudy, red-and-blue sign.

"You HAVE to be joking..." Wes heard Kiki mutter.

KIKI: Earthly marvels (part 2)

"Wow!" murmured Stan as they entered the cavernous metal building.

Kiki stared at the rolls upon rolls of carpeting, stacked high on top of one another. If *she* had to pick an 'earthly marvel' in Fairfield, she might have gone for the hospital, where babies were born and lives were saved. But instead the alien boy had opted for the Terra Firma Discount Carpet Warehouse.

"So Humans have a ritual of putting carpets in their homes. Why do they like this furry flooring so much?" said Stan, walking over to the nearest roll and running his fingers across the textured surface.

"Er, it's kind of cosy and comfy?" Kiki replied, slightly distracted by an alert on her phone.

She checked it – and with a sinking heart saw

that she'd been tagged in a post by Lola. The image was of Kiki sandwiched between Wes and Stan in the playground at lunchtime. The text underneath read **OMG!! How low can she go?** followed by a conga line of laughing emojis.

"Stan!" came Wes's voice, sounding alarmed.

Kiki glanced up to see Stan speeding off between rows of carpeting with Wes in pursuit.

"Uh-oh..." she mumbled, noticing the disapproving stares of a couple of staff members.

She set off after both boys, finally catching up with them by the back wall, where children's rugs hung from display racks. Rugs with dots, dogs and ducks, bunnies, butterflies and teddy bears. But Stan was staring at one in particular, his head tilted to the side.

"What does this represent?" he asked, staring at a baby-blue rug with a smattering of small white pentagons on it, and a red, saucer-shaped blob.

"Well, that's supposed to be space – and, um, a spaceship," Wes explained, turning to grin at Kiki. It was too funny to see a real-life boy from space looking at a kid-friendly vision of his reality.

Kiki thought so too, and held up her mobile to

snap Stan's bemused face.

"But it is a lie! The sky of the universe is not this colour, stars are not multi-pointed, and the laws of physics would not allow a pod of this shape to fly," Stan complained. "And ... what is it that you are doing, Kiki?"

Kiki's cheeks flushed as she lowered her mobile. Was Stan freaked out about her capturing his image? Was that something not allowed on his planet?

Wes was looking suddenly worried too, as if he was half expecting Stan to disintegrate the phone in Kiki's hand.

"I was just ... just taking your photo. See?" she said quickly, flipping the mobile round to show Stan the screen. "It's just for fun!"

A smile appeared on Stan's face. "It is me! As a Human Boy! I must copy this just for fun!"

He reached across, touched a finger to the screen and – with a tiny crackle – transferred the picture of himself to his data lens. Kiki could see the tiny image flickering in his eye.

"In exchange, here is a filming I did today," said Stan, keeping his finger on the phone a few seconds more.

As soon as he let go, Kiki swivelled her mobile round, wondering what Stan's 'filming' would consist of. Wes leaned in too, just as curious.

It turned out the 'filming' was of birds. Pigeons in fact. They spun in slow-motion spirals, wings wide and graceful, smooth feathers all shades of silver, steel-grey, iridescent-blue, green and mauve. Their individual sky dances merged together, like a living set of cogs all intertwined in mid-air.

"These birds are remarkable..." Stan said wistfully.

"Awesome," said Wes.

Kiki stared at both boys. Any other time, she would have laughed out loud at the idea of skanky pigeons being in any way remarkable or awesome. But Stan had certainly made them look that way. Or maybe they always had been pretty special and she'd just never noticed.

"Er, can I help you with something?" came the voice of a sales assistant, his voice dripping with sarcasm.

"Yes!" Stan burst out. "I would very much like to have ground fur for my basement!"

With the quickest of grins and glances, Kiki and

Wes grabbed an arm each and ran the Star Boy out of Terra Firma, only slowing down once they got to the car park.

"I didn't realize how late it was getting!" said Wes, checking his watch. "I'd better get home. I can drop Stan back at school on my way."

"You can wriggle through the broken fence on the riverside path, Stan," Kiki suggested.

"Yes, that is correct. And thank you – I have found everything very instructive and educational," the Star Boy said matter-of-factly. "May I be with you again tomorrow?"

"Definitely!" Wes said enthusiastically. "We could show you around some more after school. Couldn't we, Kiki?"

"Maybe," Kiki said with a shrug. "*If you're still here.*"

Her heart sank a little as she spoke. She hadn't realized what fun she'd been having till she imagined how dull and empty tomorrow would be without an alien in it...

Wednesday: How to feel at home

WES: Earthly marvels (part 3)

"Wesley!" the head teacher called out, as she stomped along the corridor that heaved with lunchtime crowds. "Outdoor coats and jackets are not to be worn inside school. How often have you been told?"

"Yes, miss," Wes mumbled, as Mrs Evans disappeared into her office.

Wes pushed back his hood, unzipped his jacket and shrugged it off. He'd barely had the chance to stuff it under his arm when it got yanked away from him.

"'How often have you been told!'" said Harvey Wickes, mimicking the head teacher's words. "Here, catch..."

He tossed the bundled jacket in the air, where it

flapped and unravelled, sending the contents of its pockets skittering and scattering across the floor. As Harvey wandered off, laughing, Wes fell to his knees, grabbing the nearest things first: keys to his flat, his inhaler, the old sixpence. The tiny star earring and shell had travelled further, and were just about to be stepped on by a tall, big-footed sixth-former when someone bent down and scooped them up.

"Here are your small objects," said Stan, passing them to Wes.

The Star Boy was wearing his crumpled school uniform, the tie twirled into a bow instead of a knot. Wes would have to fix that quick, before students started pointing and sniggering, before staff told him off, before Stan basically became too noticeable.

"You're still here!" Wes replied happily, as he took the offered earring and shell.

"Yes, that is correct. I wanted to find you and tell you I was not yet rescued in the night-time."

"Sorry – I meant to check on you earlier, but I was late for school this morning, and I got detention at break..."

Wes had stayed up stupidly late, watching out of his window for telltale signs of any rescue craft in the night sky. He'd slept through his alarm, been shaken awake by his dad, and run off to school leaving his homework behind, which had gone down pretty badly with his maths teacher.

"I have been adequately busy this morning, so do not concern yourself," said Stan, getting to his feet, with Wes beside him. "I worked for quite some time on the communication device in the pod – it is gratifyingly showing some signs of life."

"That's good," said Wes, holding his mum-treasures tight in his fist.

"And I also studied Human emotions to broaden my understanding," Stan carried on earnestly. "On *my* planet, we have a limited range of emotions, but *you* have a bewildering amount to choose from. I now know how to recognize and apply many of them. For example, there is 'dislike'. And that boy who always treats you in a negative way? I *dislike* him."

"Me too," grinned Wes. "But listen, I'm just on my way to the music room to rehearse. Are you coming?"

"Yes, I am *excited* and *ecstatic* to see Kiki again," said Stan, as they headed off in the direction of the music department. "And I am *delighted* to tell you that I know which earthly marvel I wish to see today."

Wes couldn't wait to find out what was next on Stan's alien bucket list. What could be better than a trip on a bus and a visit to a warehouse in the retail park...?

KIKI: Say nothing and smile

The rehearsal was good. Much to their joint surprise, Kiki's ukulele and Wes's drums wove together really well, as if they'd been playing together for a lot longer than two lunchtimes.

It *had* taken a while for Kiki to feel confident enough to sing, even longer to sing with her head up and not staring shyly at the floor, but she got there.

After a few ever-improving run-throughs, Kiki and Wes ended their most confident performance to applause from Mr McKenzie, who'd quietly slipped into the music room, along with a too-loud, "THIS IS VERY GOOD! IT MAKES ME HAPPY!" from an overly excited Stan.

And Stan was obviously feeling very good, very

happy and also slightly overexcited again now.

Kiki sat side by side on the sofa with Wes, school bags dumped by their feet, both gazing up at him.

"I am *surprised* and *charmed* by this sensation!" Stan announced, as he stomped barefoot round Kiki's living room, scrunching his toes in the thick pile of the carpet.

"I can tell," said Kiki, with a raised eyebrow and a smile.

Stan was experiencing his third earthly marvel: seeing a genuine furry floor covering inside a real Human home. Wes had straight away ruled out going to *his* flat because his dad would be busy at his computer in the living room. So it had been a no-brainer for Kiki to have Stan and Wes back to her flat, since Mum was at work and Eddie and Ty were at the park, testing the wonky drone.

"Come! Join me! It will make you feel *joyful*!" said Stan, bending down and yanking a shoe from Wes's foot.

"Hey! Stop!" Wes protested, as Kiki burst out laughing.

At the same time, it occurred to her how totally unexpected it was to be laughing and goofing around with Wes. After all, only a few weeks ago – the morning after the first unexpected storm – she had been sitting on this very sofa, watching him being interviewed on TV.

Kiki gave a little shudder of shame, remembering the snarky message she'd sent her so-called friends about Wes. Never in a zillion years could she have imagined hanging out with him here in her living room, along with an alien who'd been involved in causing the storm in the first place...

"OK, OK!" Wes laughingly agreed, taking off the other shoe and both socks and getting to his feet.

"Nope!" Kiki shrieked again, this time because Stan was making a move on her Kickers. She wriggled her feet away from his fingers and jumped off the sofa to get away from him. "No way! Stop!"

"I am *perplexed*. Why will you not have fun, Kiki?" Stan asked her.

Kiki paused at that question. Why *didn't* she want to have fun? Was it a hangover from her friendship with Lola and the other girls? Was it something about having to be cool all the time?

"Fine! I'll have fun!" Kiki announced, quickly untangling the double knots of her laces. In ten seconds flat, she'd yanked off her boots and black knee socks and was barefoot beside both the boys.

"This is very pleasurable," said Stan, pad-pad-padding round the room. "I cannot understand why Humans do not choose to do pleasurable things at all times. Why do they sometimes choose to do dislikeable things? Like the Human Girls who did sneers to you, Kiki, and that Human Boy today, Wes..."

Kiki stopped wriggling her toes in the tufts of carpet and looked up.

"What happened?" she asked.

"The Human Boy with a face like this –" Stan pulled a quick sneer – "took Wes's jacket and threw it far away. I helped Wes pick up his small objects from the ground."

"Was it Harvey Wilkes again?" Kiki asked Wes.

"Yeah," said Wes, with a little shoulder shrug. "But it doesn't really bother me."

"How can it not bother you?" asked Kiki incredulously. It had been a whole day, and she was still *really* bothered about the mean post Lola had put up on Instagram – *and* its zillion likes – not to mention the continued silent treatment from her former friends, which everyone was still talking about.

Wes hesitated for a second, as if he was deciding to say something or not.

"When my mum and dad split up, it was the *worst* feeling," he finally muttered. "After that ... I guess nothing could hurt as bad. So I decided that if someone teased me, or hassled me, I'd just let it bounce right off."

"Like a force field!" said Stan.

Wes grinned. "Something like that. It's not exactly a sci-fi superpower, although I wish it was sometimes!"

"Must be kind of useful when it comes to dealing with real-life idiots, though," Kiki suggested, wishing she could develop a force field of her own.

"Were your small objects damaged?" she heard Stan say to Wes.

Kiki looked puzzled. "What small objects?" she asked.

"I know this is going to sound stupid, but when my mum left I kept hold of a few things of hers," Wes said sheepishly.

Kiki stared at him for a second, her heart pitter-pattering with recognition.

"Why do you say this is 'stupid'?" she heard Stan ask, sounding perplexed. "I learned that Humans like to collect things. They find this *satisfying* not stupid, I think?"

"Like mementos," Kiki said directly to Wes, ignoring Stan's question.

"Yeah, like mementos," Wes answered, holding Kiki's gaze. "Here..."

He rummaged in his inside pocket, then got off the sofa and knelt on the floor, gently placing his three treasures on the coffee table. Kiki and Stan crouched down beside him.

"This is one of Mum's favourite earrings; I found it in a crack between the floorboards years after she left," said Wes, pointing to the small silver star. "And see this old sixpence? That was something Mum's granny gave her for luck. And then *this* –"

He held up the pinky-white shell.

"– I found on the beach when we were on holiday, when I was about five. I gave it to my mum and she was so pleased. She hugged me like it was the most amazing present ever, as if it was as rare as a pearl or something."

"I don't fully understand," said Stan, pointing to the smooth shell as he carefully studied Wes's face. "This particular collectible object makes you *happy* or *sad*?"

"A bit of both." Wes shrugged, his pale cheeks flushing.

Kiki felt a sharp ache in her chest for him. The shell hadn't meant as much to his mum as Wes thought; not enough to take with her. A bit like him?

"Anyway, sorry..." said Wes, giving himself a shake, looking shy and awkward. "I told you it was going to sound stupid."

"No, it doesn't," said Kiki, getting to her feet. "Back in a sec..."

After running to her room and quickly rifling through the bottom drawer of her bedside table, Kiki returned and spread out her saved things next to Wes's.

"This was my dad's old CD Walkman, with this compilation CD he made inside – 'What a Wonderful World' is on there. This is his old bus pass; I just really like his smile in that photo. And this really IS going to sound dumb, but here's one of his old asthma inhalers. When I was little, he used to pull funny faces when he was using one, so I didn't get worried about him."

"Maybe I should start doing that!" Wes joked, pulling out his own inhaler and crossing his eyes.

Kiki smiled, feeling a little giddy. She'd never shown these useless but precious things to anyone before. Not even Vic and Megan, since they'd seemed really uncomfortable and not known what to say to her when her dad moved out. But after Wes going first, sharing her own junk treasures had been OK, *good* even.

"So how long ago did your parents split up?" she asked Wes.

"Five years," said Wes. "What about you?"

"About a year ago," Kiki replied.

She found they were smiling at each other, both understanding their hurt in common without having to explain it to each other. She hadn't realized Wes was so sensitive. But then she hadn't realized a lot of things about him, like how funny and sweet he could be. Wes kept a lot of himself hidden away under that hood of his...

"These images enclosed in wood and glass – these are collectible objects too?" Kiki heard Stan ask now. She looked up to see him pointing to a row of framed photos on the shelves beside the TV.

"Yes, I suppose they are," Kiki agreed, bouncing up to grab one and show him. "Here's one of my mum and me and my brother Tyreke from the summer holidays."

"Your mum and brother," murmured Stan. "They are nice Humans?"

"I wouldn't go THAT FAR!" said Kiki. "Mum's OK but I'm sometimes pretty tempted to swap Ty for a better brother. Or a dog. Or even just a *picture* of a dog."

Stan blinked at her, trying to understand her meaning.

"This is *humour*, yes?" he asked, keen to improve his working knowledge of Human interaction, as well as Human emotions. "You do not genuinely mean to change your brother for a piece of paper with a canine printed on it?"

"Some days I would," replied Kiki.

She suddenly noticed that Wes was staring at her, grinning.

"What?" she challenged him.

"Nothing!" he said with a shrug. "You're just

really funny, that's all!"

VROOOOM!

"Uh-oh," muttered Kiki, recognizing the rumble and clatter of a rickety motorbike pulling up outside. She hadn't expected Eddie and Ty to be home so soon.

"Uh-oh... Is this a *bad* thing, Kiki?" Stan asked, his eyes wide. "Are we in danger?"

"No! It's fine," Kiki said hastily, hearing Ty and Eddie's voices outside the front door. "But I don't think you should stick around. Ty saw space pods in the sky during the big storm, remember? Maybe he'll somehow *know* you're not human!"

"*How* would he know?" Wes whispered anxiously.

"I don't know! But I don't want to risk it – do you?" Kiki challenged him, as she heard the door whack open and the thump of crash helmets and shoes being dumped.

"No ... course not," said Wes, gathering up his treasures and hurrying to put on his socks and shoes. "I'll take Stan back to school."

"Good. And Stan – don't talk, just smile and leave, OK?" Kiki ordered the alien, as she grabbed her backpack and stuffed her own treasures inside it.

"OK." Stan nodded nervously, as hellos. and footsteps sounded from the hall.

"And definitely DON'T do that with your eyes!" Kiki snapped at him.

"You're blinking in the wrong direction again," Wes pitched in helpfully.

"I apologize," Stan said hurriedly, and just as hurriedly squirmed his eyelids the right way round before two smiling people bounded into the living room.

"I'm Ty! Why are YOU two here? I don't know you!" Ty blurted out.

"Hi, Kiki! Hi, guys!" said an unfazed Eddie, rubbing his hand through Ty's hair. "Ty's starving so I'm going to start cooking. Are your friends staying for tea?"

"No, they're not staying. And they're not *really* friends," said Kiki quickly. Too quickly.

She felt heat flare in her cheeks at the sound of her cutting words and didn't know how to backtrack. She stared at the floor, unable to look at Wes and Stan, not wanting to see their reaction.

Why had she said that? Kiki wondered to herself. Maybe it was because the last couple of days had been pretty head-melting. The stuff going on with Lola had made her completely miserable. At the same time, coming across Stan had been beyond amazing.

And the last hour? Kiki had had the best time since ... since she could remember. Still, she'd only known Wes and Stan for two days. And Wes wasn't exactly the sort of person she'd normally hang out with, while Stan wasn't a person at *all* so they couldn't *technically* be described as friends, could they?

In the space of a few seconds, Kiki's thoughts flipped back and forth till she felt dizzy.

"What are they doing here if they're NOT your friends?" Ty demanded, as Eddie lolloped off to the kitchen.

"I didn't mean that exactly," Kiki waffled, tying herself up in knots. "They just came to talk about performing at my school's Open Evening tomorrow."

"*They* are performing. *I* am not performing – that is an untruth," Stan burst in brightly, while Kiki quietly wilted at his words. He'd forgotten her instructions to say nothing and just smile.

"Uh, whatever," said Ty. "I was at the park just now.

Do YOU like the park?"

Wes gave a vague nod. Stan instantly tried to copy him, bobbing his head like a jiggly toy.

"I got crisps at the café," Ty babbled on. "They were prawn cocktail flavour. What type of crisps are YOUR favourite?"

"Um, cheese and onion?" Wes said, sounding confused by the whirling, unstoppable force that was Ty.

"And YOURS?" he demanded of Stan.

"Cheesy ... um-yums?" the Star Boy said hesitantly.

"OK, that's enough," Kiki told Ty. "Say bye to Wes and Stan – they're going."

"Bye!" Ty yelled distractedly, already leaping on to the sofa and grabbing the TV remote.

"Nice to meet you! Maybe see you around?" said Eddie, sticking his head out of the kitchen as he heard the front door opening.

I doubt it, thought Kiki, as she motioned Wes and Stan to leave, still finding it hard to make eye contact with the boys.

"Um, so see you tomorrow lunchtime for the last rehearsal?" she heard Wes say.

"Yeah, sure," Kiki replied, hoping she was

forgiven for her tactless words.

She glanced up, and watched Wes and Stan set off down the road.

"I like your mum! She is very kind and friendly!" Stan suddenly called back over his shoulder to Kiki. "But she looks different from the photograph you showed me…"

Kiki frowned, then a smile spread across her face. She was about to shout back and explain that Eddie *wasn't* in fact her mother, but kept quiet. Instead of alerting the whole street to Stan's not-of-this-world confusion, she would explain what childminders were when she saw him the next day.

IF he's still here tomorrow, Kiki realized, her smile slip-sliding away as she shut the front door.

Could that have been the last time she ever saw him? Should she run after him and Wes and say a proper goodbye, just in case?

A jangle from Kiki's mobile interrupted that thought. Grabbing the phone from her pocket, she half expected to see a message from Wes, a quick post about how funny Stan's comment was. But then she remembered that she and Wes hadn't swapped numbers. When Stan was gone, they'd have nothing in common.

Hey, let's talk, she read on the screen.

It was from someone she hadn't expected to speak to ever again.

Lola.

Thursday: Enemies at close range

STAR BOY: Show-and-tell

The Star Boy examined the collectible objects he'd gently placed on the Terra Firma sign. They consisted of:

- *a ridged wooden oval called an acorn*
- *a soft, stretchy circle of cloth known as a scrunchie*
- *a five-pence piece that reminded him of Wes's silver coin*
- *an enormous, empty tin cylinder with fat red fruit printed on a paper label, with the words Tomatoes: Catering Can*
- *a rustling plastic envelope that once contained cheesy um-yum crisps*
- *a small, flat, blackened and burnt something.*

The Star Boy had selected and gathered the

objects in the soft dawn light, after a night spent in the pod, tinkering with the electronics, learning the words to 'What a Wonderful World', and listening to the distant hums and crackles of space through the patchily working communication device.

He'd found the acorn, the scrunchie and the crisp envelope in the undergrowth. The five pence had been dropped near the large bins-on-wheels. The huge can had been *in* one of the large bins, alongside lots of old, soggy Human food. What a find! As for the blackened and burnt something...

BE-ZINGGG! BE-ZINGGG!

The jarring sound of the school bell alerted the Star Boy to the fact that it was now lunching-time. As he gently morphed from glowing amber to an acceptable Human shade, he began to put on his school-uniform disguise. Wes had arranged to meet him – if the Star Boy hadn't been rescued in the meantime – so that they could walk into school together, and head for the music room and the final rehearsal.

The Star Boy was *excited*. He couldn't wait to be like a real Human again, to be 'Stan', to listen to Wes and Kiki making their song happen. He couldn't wait to show them his own collectible objects, which were just as lovely and interesting as theirs.

And the Star Boy couldn't wait to see his friends' faces when he explained the story behind one particular item...

KIKI: To walk away or stay

It was the very start of lunch break, but Kiki kept checking the time on her phone. She knew that she and her sandwich should be up in the music room right now, but instead she was perched, alone and self-conscious, on the picnic bench in the playground.

Kiki had been summoned to wait here by Lola's text message the day before. She had no clue about what Lola might say. Yesterday's **Hey, let's talk. Usual bench tomorrow lunchtime** DM didn't give much away.

She nibbled at her nails. Kiki had only come because the part of her that believed in fairness was hoping that Lola might be about to apologize. To say sorry to Kiki for overreacting to an accident, to make up for blanking her so brutally this week. (If that happened, would Lola follow up by asking if they could still be friends? In spite of lying awake all night, Kiki still hadn't figured out how she'd feel if that happened...)

Of course, the flipside was that Lola might be in the mood for ramping things up with some face-to-face humiliation. It was possible; she and Zainab and Saffron hadn't made any effort to speak to Kiki during classes this morning. Maybe Kiki was about to get shouted at? Told what a loser she was?

Whichever way this went, Kiki hoped it wouldn't take too long. She glanced again at the time on her phone. Wes and Stan would be waiting and wondering where she was – if Stan was still on planet Earth, and not halfway home to wherever he came from, she realized with a twinge of sadness.

But, with one more triangular glance at the digital display on her watch, the upstairs window of the music room and back down to the double doors where Lola was likely to come out, Kiki began to lose her nerve.

Should she walk away? Or stay?

Walk away?

Stay?

"Walk away!" Kiki finally muttered to herself, reaching down for her rucksack.

"Oi!"

Lola's shout made her jump, and Kiki glanced up to see a formidable group of people coming towards her: Lola, Zainab and Saffron, trailed by Harvey, Jake, Jarek and Archie kicking an empty plastic bottle to each other.

Kiki let go of her bag, and took a deep breath.

WES: From friend to *un*-friend?

Wes awkwardly drummed his fingers on the bongos, stopping and starting, and stopping again.

"Stupid fingers aren't working," he joked to Stan, holding his hands up. "Don't know what's wrong with me..."

But Wes *did* know. Rehearsing without Kiki singing and strumming beside him didn't seem right. Something else not right was the uncomfortable feeling he'd had since they left Kiki's flat yesterday, after that comment she'd made in front of her brother about him and Stan not *really* being her friends. He didn't have any right to think of her as a friend, he supposed, but after the fun they'd had with Stan and his earthly marvels, after sharing their mementos and little bits of their stories...

"Does this help?" he heard Stan ask.

The Star Boy had turned away from the window he'd been staring out of and flicked his thumb, sending a fine bolt flying from the tip of it to the nearest computer. YouTube instantly launched, and the opening bars of 'What a Wonderful World' began.

"Yep, that definitely helps, thanks," said Wes, lowering his hands back down to the smooth skin surface of the bongos and picking up the beat.

"I listened to this song in the night-time, many times over. I like the words very much," said Stan, staring back out at the drifting clouds. "They are happy words, about nature and rainbows and friends and how good it is to be a Human. Yes?"

"Um, yes," Wes agreed, never having given much thought to the lyrics himself. But he liked Stan's optimism, and didn't bother mentioning that there were lots of Human songs with gloomier sorts of lyrics.

"Kiki is late," Stan suddenly announced. "Perhaps she is dead or injured?"

"What?" Wes said with some alarm.

"We were taught that Human lifespans are short,

with most not living beyond one hundred years," said Stan.

Wes's head spun, but he was quick to reassure the Star Boy.

"Kiki's nowhere near a hundred. I'm sure she'll be here soon. There was probably just a really long queue at the sandwich counter."

At least he *hoped* she'd be here.

"A long queue ... a sandwich..." Stan repeated, sounding as if he was scrolling through his data lens. "Ah, I understand. But I wish Kiki would come soon. I want to show you both something that will cause you *surprise*."

"Yeah?" said Wes, intrigued. He was about to ask for a clue at least when Mr McKenzie stuck his head round the classroom door.

"Hi, Wes!" the teacher called out cheerfully. "And hi ... um..."

Mr McKenzie stumbled, looking at Stan and trying to remember his name.

"Stan BOYD. STAN Boyd. STAN!" the Star Boy announced cheerily to the teacher, still not quite settled on the best pronunciation of his Human name.

"Stan ... right," replied Mr McKenzie. "So how're rehearsals going? Where's Kiki?"

"Fine. She's just running late," said Wes.

"She is NOT dead," added Stan.

"Well, that's a relief!" laughed Mr McKenzie. "Anyway, about the Open Evening – Mrs Evans' talk is at six p.m., so come to the hall just before that to get set up. Oh, and here are some guest passes for your families, so they can come and watch you perform."

"My dad's busy – he won't be able to come," Wes said straight away. He didn't mean to lie; the fact was that Dad didn't like going out if he could help it. He'd always been a bit like that, and even more so since Mum left. But it was hard explaining it to people, so Wes found a fib the easier option.

"No worries. Well, here're a few for Kiki," said Mr McKenzie, handing a bunch of tickets to Wes. "How about you, Stan? Fancy coming along and cheering on your new friends?"

"Yes, that would make me *ecstatic*!" said Stan.

"Great, well, you can't fault a bit of enthusiasm!" said Mr McKenzie, handing a ticket to Stan. "Right, look forward to seeing you later..."

As Mr McKenzie closed the door, Stan spoke up.

"I see Kiki! She is not eating a sandwich. She is sitting in the Outside with the Human Girls who *enjoy* being horrible..."

Wes plonked his bongos on the chair and hurried over to Stan's side.

And there was Kiki ... looking very settled on the picnic bench with Lola whatshername and her friends. Harvey Wilkes and his mates were mucking about together close by.

In that moment, Wes realized – with a sinking heart – that Kiki probably wasn't coming.

KIKI: Forgiven – sort of

"So," Lola began, plonking her big handbag down on the table and sliding on to the wooden seat across from Kiki. "I've decided to forgive you."

Three sets of eyes were fixed on Kiki, waiting for her grateful response. Her brain whirled madly, trying to process how she felt. It WAS an apology, but only sort of...

"Just don't be a dork again, OK?" said Lola, holding out a small tub of chewing gum.

Was this an actual invitation to rejoin the Popular Crew? Stuck for words, Kiki couldn't think of what to do apart from help herself to a piece of gum.

"And anyway we're fed up with Bilal sitting with us," said Zainab. "He keeps trying to talk to us. We need you back in your spot."

Wait – they wanted to be friends again because they liked and had missed her ... or just because Kiki was less boring than Bilal?

"Yeah, and –" Saffron leaned forward to whisper something, while nodding towards the boys playing kickabout close by – "we're hanging out with Harvey and the boys more. There're four of them, so it makes sense if there are four of us."

Kiki wasn't sure that made *any* kind of sense.

"Anyway, the main thing is I need your help, Kiki," said Lola, leaning her chin on her hand and gazing intently at Kiki.

Kiki stopped chewing her gum. Part of her had been tempted to tell Lola that after being dumped, ignored, sneered at and made a fool of, she didn't care about 'being forgiven'. But the other part of her couldn't help but feel flattered. The most popular girl of the most popular crew in Year Seven needed her help. Kiki felt the warmth, the comfort of belonging, begin to wash over her.

"What do you need me to do?" she asked.

"Right, so Miss Amari sent me to Mrs Evans because I wouldn't spit out my gum," Lola began with a roll of her eyes. "And Mrs Evans gave me a choice: detention or helping out at the Open Evening tonight. I've got to be on the door and hand out stupid info sheets to parents FOR TWO HOURS."

Lola paused. Kiki frowned, not sure what Lola was trying to say, or how exactly Lola thought she could help.

"Well, I'm not going to do *anything* that embarrassing on my *own*, am I?" Lola announced.

"*I* can't be there – my auntie and cousins are coming for tea," said Zainab.

"And *I've* got the dentist, Kiki," said Saffron. "So *you* have to help Lola."

The warmth she'd felt cooled a little. So *that* was what this was about: Kiki was Lola's last resort...

"Yeah, but I'm busy too," said Kiki. "I've got to do something at the Open Evening anyway."

"Like what?" demanded Lola.

"Mr McKenzie asked me to perform after Mrs Evans' speech, so..."

"Yeah? Well, that'll work," said Lola, leaning back and rattling the tub of chewing gum in the direction of the boys. "You and me have to be on the door at four p.m. Mrs Evans' speech isn't till six p.m. So that's sorted."

"What do you mean you're 'performing', Kiki?" asked Saffron.

Kiki felt prickles of awkwardness ripple up and down her spine. She was just going to mutter something about Wes partnering her when Harvey barged into the conversation.

"You saying you're going to be at the Open Evening, Kiki?" he asked her.

"Um, yeah ... why?" she replied, startled that Harvey was even talking to her. She waited for him to follow up with a sarky comment, but it didn't come.

"Did you know Mrs Evans is getting *me* to talk?" he said, pushing his chest out like a preening pigeon. "It's cos I'm the Year Seven football captain and—"

"Hey, guys ... guys!" Zainab interrupted Harvey's boasting. "Check out who's coming over!"

Kiki heard the groans from the boys, and the giggles from the girls. Turning round, she felt sick... Wes and Stan were walking straight towards them.

Conflicting thoughts rattled round her head again. She'd been wrong to judge Wes – he was pretty sweet and funny, and Stan was too, as well as being an actual ALIEN. But right at this second, with their nearly matching Puffa jackets and hoods firmly up, they looked pretty odd and more than a little bit embarrassing.

"Hey, Wesley – who's your friend?" Harvey asked loudly.

Wes didn't respond to Harvey. He waved at Stan to stop and stay back, then approached the bench. Like an obedient dog, Stan stayed where he was, his eyes scanning everyone round the picnic table, Kiki noticed.

"Mr McKenzie asked me to give you these," said Wes, holding out the guest passes. "In case your mum and brother want to come and see us tonight."

"*Us?*" Kiki heard Lola say. "What does he mean, Kiki? OMG, you're not doing a song with *him*, are you?"

"Are you coming to rehearse?" Wes asked Kiki, ignoring Lola's snidey comment.

"No, she's not!" Lola said very definitely. "We're having a conversation so go away!"

Wes blink-blinked at Kiki. Kiki couldn't hold his glance, and instead stared down at the passes in her hand.

She felt terrible, and didn't expect Wes to understand. She could barely believe she was about to blank him the way she'd been blanked herself this week. But, if she walked away with him and Stan now, the teasing and mean comments would get much, *much* worse. It had suddenly, sadly dawned on Kiki that she could be shunned for the rest of her school life.

So even if she didn't totally trust Lola and the other girls, even if she wasn't sure she even *liked* them right at this second, Kiki knew in her heart of hearts that it was safer being *in* the Popular Crew than out of it.

"See you, losers!" Harvey called out, alerting Kiki to the fact that Wes and Stan were going. She snuck a quick look at them as guilt, sadness and relief crushed together in her chest.

No wonder Stan finds human emotions so hard to understand, thought Kiki, feeling like a coward and a failure…

WES: Repeat, please!

Wes's force field wasn't working very well. The hurt of Kiki blanking him hadn't bounced off. It had seeped through his jacket and left him with a soggy ache across his shoulders.

"Why has Kiki become unfriendly towards us?" Stan asked him, as they zigzagged through the chatting crowds of students in the playground.

"I don't know," said Wes, hurrying, but not sure where to. Not back inside the building, not back to the music room. What was the point?

"Kiki is not unpleasant. So why has she chosen the company of these unpleasant people?" Stan continued with his quest to understand.

"They used to be her friends. I think she fell out with them, but they've obviously made up again,"

Wes mumbled.

"I remember the Master told us that Humans like to belong in groups. It is healthy for them," said Stan. "But how can it be healthy to belong to a group that is unkind and unlike you?"

"Don't ask me," muttered Wes, as the crowds thinned out now that they were closer to the lower playground. "I've never had a group to belong to. I'm used to being on my own. Like I will be when you leave."

Stan pushed his hood from his head and smiled broadly at Wes.

"Wes, I have something I must tell you," he said excitedly.

"What is it?" asked Wes, wondering if he should be worried.

"It would be better if I showed you," said Stan. "May you come with me to my down-below room?"

Wes glanced around – no students were remotely interested in the two boys or what they were doing (including Kiki, obviously).

"Yeah, come on then," said Wes, hurrying down towards the lower playground and Stan's basement hideout.

Barely a minute or two later, Wes watched as the door-locking mechanism clunked open without Stan laying a finger on the handle. Next, he followed his friend inside, and heard the hum of machinery in the low-ceilinged room and noticed the gloom that clung to the edges of Stan's temporary home. They didn't dare turn the light on in case it was noticed. But Stan had begun to shed his human shape, and his Star Boy amber glow lit up the collected items he had spread out over the top of the generator.

That's when Stan finally spilled his news.

He was going nowhere.

"You've done what?" Wes asked, staring into the Star Boy's liquid-black eyes and feeling the hairs on his arms start to prickle.

"You wish me to repeat this information?" Stan asked.

"Yes!" said Wes, blink-blinking furiously.

"I was going to show you and Kiki *this* at lunching-time, but she was with her Others," said Stan.

"Yeah, I know that bit," said Wes. "I meant *this*! And what it means!"

Wes was pointing to the small blackened item placed near the torn crisp packet.

"It is my pod's location alerter," said Stan. "In the night-time, I downloaded some information about how I might repair it at last. And then I decided I did not want to. So I destroyed it instead."

Wes poked the burnt, rock-hard lump.

"You definitely *don't* want to be rescued?" he checked.

"No. I am fascinated by nothing on my planet, and everything on Earth. There is no one to miss me on my planet, and here I have friends!"

One friend at least, thought Wes, fleetingly recalling Kiki's traitorous choice to stay with the populars earlier.

"But there's still your pod," said Wes, returning to more pressing matters. "Are you going to keep the invisibility shield *permanently* switched on?"

"Unfortunately, it keeps malfunctioning," said Stan. "So I am currently researching how to safely destroy all traces of my pod."

Wes's fingers drum-drummed against his leg, other questions and worries trying to sort themselves out and make themselves heard. Questions and worries like how could Stan live in the basement permanently? Mr Shah was bound to come down here now and again. If the site manager came across the bundle of school uniform and Stan's random bits and pieces, things could get complicated...

The harsh *zing!* of the school bell cut through the tangled wires of Wes's thoughts.

"You must go," said Stan. "But you will come for me later? And take me to your performance?"

"Stan, I don't think Kiki wants to do it any more," Wes cautioned him, as he walked towards the door.

"But it is equally possible that she might!" Stan said enthusiastically, his glow brightening.

Wes gave him an unconvinced shrug in reply and quickly left, before he ended up being late for afternoon classes.

Would Kiki show up? he wondered, as he hurried up the steps, pulling his hood over his head. It was a big question. Wes didn't know how he'd react if she came, not after how she'd behaved earlier. But he also knew he'd be gutted if she didn't.

And then another big question crossed his mind.

He and Kiki shared a HUGE secret.

Was Kiki going to keep it?

KIKI: Being heard

The hall was packed, primary pupils and their adults all listening attentively to Mrs Evans as she strode about the stage. Dull graphs about results popped up on the screen above her head, while behind her various mic stands and musical equipment sat waiting for the rap band, the saxophonist, and Kiki and Wes...

"I wish Mrs Evans would hurry up – I want to see Harvey do his talk," Lola muttered to Kiki, cracking gum noisily between her teeth. With the tours finally over, and the info sheets all gone, the girls were hovering at the back of the hall, Lola's arm hooked into Kiki's.

Kiki's attention was on two *different* boys. Wes and Stan were easy to spot with their hoods up;

Wes was in the front row with the other performers – including Harvey, sitting next to him – and Stan was in the second row, directly behind Wes. Stan had already turned and smiled at Kiki several times, his niceness making her feel pretty awful. As for Wes... He'd kept his focus on the stage, never once looking round.

After how she'd treated him, Kiki had half expected Wes not to turn up at the Open Evening. All afternoon, she'd hoped to see him in the corridors, to say or at least *smile* a quick apology, but had had no luck spotting him. Kiki hadn't even seen him come into the main reception area while she was handing out the info sheets.

Then it occurred to her: was Wes sitting wondering if *she* still wanted to do the song with him? It had seemed such a cringy idea when Mr McKenzie first suggested it, but Kiki definitely wanted to go through with it now. After all, performing 'What a Wonderful World' with Wes could be the best way to apologize, better than any clumsy words she might come up with.

"Hey, who did you say that geeky-looking guy is with your mum and brother?" Kiki heard Lola ask.

Kiki let out a little sigh, and looked over at Ty, currently wriggling and squiggling in his chair, clunking his lightsabre against its legs. It was bad enough that Mum had been so keen to come along tonight, after Kiki had phoned her and told her about the tickets, but worse that she'd brought Ty and Eddie with her, as if Eddie was part of the family. Kiki watched as Eddie handed his phone to Ty, in an effort to distract him with some game.

"That's Eddie. He sometimes looks after my brother," she whispered in reply. She'd forgotten how little Lola knew about her life. To be honest, her friend had never seemed particularly interested.

As if to prove the point, Lola's attention had already switched elsewhere.

"It looks like Harvey's getting ready for his speech!" she said admiringly, as Harvey sat up, running his hands through his hair.

In that moment, Kiki realized that as soon as Harvey left for the stage, there'd be an empty seat next to Wes.

"I have to go," she murmured, uncoupling her arm from Lola's.

She quickly headed towards the front row,

hugging the wall on the way so she wouldn't disturb anyone. As she walked, she saw Harvey get to his feet – and accidentally-on-purpose elbow Wes on the side of the head. Someone let out a snort of stifled laughter; someone who sounded very like Lola.

Mrs Evans welcomed Harvey onstage while Kiki slipped into his newly vacated seat. She turned to give Stan a quick smile, but his hood was facing the back of the hall, as if he was trying to locate the source of the laughter.

With her heart pounding, she focused on Wes.

"Hi," she whispered.

"Hi," he muttered, not looking at her. She heard his breathing, though – it was wheezy and fast. No wonder, after what Harvey had just done.

"I saw that," she said in a voice so low only Wes could hear. "Harvey's an idiot."

And so am I, she reminded herself.

"Wes, I'm sorry about lunchtime, but—"

Wes whipped his head round, his moon face earnest and worried.

"Are you going to tell?" he interrupted her whispered apology, looking as if the entire future safety of the world depended on her answer.

"Tell who what?" she said softly, suddenly thrown by how pale and serious Wes was looking.

"Are you going to tell Lola and everyone about Stan?" he whispered urgently.

Kiki's heart sank. Did Wes *really* believe she would do something that awful? Risk Stan's safety for the sake of a bit of gossip? But why *wouldn't* he think she'd do that, after the way she'd behaved?

"What? No! I would never—"

"Shh!" someone's parent hissed from behind. Kiki did as she was told and shushed. Up on the stage, Harvey stood beside Mrs Evans with a cocky grin on his face.

"You'll find out all about our school clubs in a minute, and be hearing from the captain of our Year Seven football team. But first let's have a look at the sort of welcome your child can expect from everyone here at Riverside!" said Mrs Evans, pointing her clicker at the overhead projector.

Kiki remembered this section from last year; it consisted of a lot of slides featuring various smiley students and teachers, plus cheery lunchtime serving staff waving their ladles. It was a bit of a cheat, Kiki had come to realize. It wasn't as if 'everyone' was welcoming, or that secondary school was a big, happy hug-a-thon all the time. But she bet the ever-optimistic Stan would like it, and turned to see his reaction.

Except Stan appeared to be up to something, flicking his thumb in the direction of the projector, his gaze – hidden by his hood from those on either side of him – fixed on it.

Uh-oh...

Kiki heard gasps from the audience and looked back up at the screen. Like the quick *flip-flip-flip* of Stories on Instagram, Stan was downloading every image his data lens had recorded of Harvey and Lola and their crews over the last few days. Every sneer, scowl and snarl, every mean act – every nasty whisper behind hands and shady look thrown – was there for all to see.

His mouth gaping, Harvey stood frozen at Mrs Evans' side as she frantically pressed the buttons on the remote. But instead of the slides pausing, a clip popped up of Harvey thunking Wes on the head with his elbow just minutes before, with the 'camera' swerving round to catch Lola cracking up with laughter at the back of the hall.

Kiki glanced quickly at Wes, and saw a small smile quiver at the corner of his mouth.

"Can you please stop the PowerPoint, Mr Smith!" Mrs Evans called out sharply to the shrugging, red-faced tech teacher hunkered over a laptop. At the same time, Mrs Evans flapped her arm at Harvey, shooing him from the stage.

"Stan!" Kiki said urgently, leaning over the back of her chair and beckoning the Star Boy closer to her. "I think you should stop now!"

"I have done enough?" Stan bent forwards and whispered. "Is it clear to that Boy and that Girl that their actions are not a correct way to be a successful Human?"

"Yeah, definitely," said Wes, turning round to join in the hushed conversation, as rumbles of unsettled surprise rose from the audience around them.

"Then I shall desist," said the Star Boy, lowering his hand and sitting back in his chair. The screen went blank.

"Apologies for that technical hitch!" said Mrs Evans, leaning into the microphone. "That was just a piece from the, er, drama department that was played in error. But let's dive straight into some music. Can we welcome to the stage ... er..."

"Kiki and Wes!" Mr McKenzie called out to the flustered head teacher from behind the curtain at the side of the stage.

"Yes, come on up, Kiki and Wes!" said Mrs Evans, desperately trying to regain control of the situation.

Kiki gulped. Not only was she going to have to get up in front of an entire audience, she was going to have to perform side by side with someone who was barely talking to her.

"So are we going to do this?" she asked Wes, with a small and shy half-smile.

But it slipped away when Kiki noticed that Wes's chest was heaving, his mouth a small 'o' as he tried to draw long, controlled draughts of air into his struggling lungs. From Mrs Evans' perspective, looking down from the stage, Wes probably just seemed nervous. Stan seemed to be more concerned.

"Is Wes injured? Will he die?" he asked, leaning in between his two human friends.

"He'll be fine, Stan – he just needs some medicine for his asthma," Kiki muttered quickly, while motioning to Mrs Evans and Mr McKenzie that they'd need a minute. "You *have* got your inhaler, haven't you, Wes?"

Wes nodded, already pulling the blue canister from his jacket pocket, giving it a quick shake before putting it to his mouth. Kiki was relieved to see him visibly relax within seconds of starting to breathe in his meds. And then she burst out laughing as Wes crossed his eyes and pulled a funny face at her.

He'd remembered the silly story about her dad! How he always pulled a face when he was using his inhaler so that she wouldn't worry. Wes wanted her not to worry ... about his asthma, and possibly about her being such an idiot too.

In that moment, Kiki knew that hanging out with Wes – and Stan too – made her a million times happier than being with so-called friends that made her nervous and on edge all the time.

"Hey, guys – need a few minutes?" said Mr McKenzie, quickly trotting down the stairs from the stage to check in with them. "One of the other acts can go first."

Wes shook his head, already sticking the inhaler back in his pocket. "We're OK, aren't we, Kiki?"

"Yes, we're OK," she agreed, with a proper wide smile this time.

And a blur of a moment later, Kiki found herself gazing out at the audience as she adjusted the strap of the ukulele, with Wes on the chair next to her, the drums on his lap. She saw Mum beaming with pride, Eddie with a big, goofy grin of encouragement, while Ty was too immersed in whatever game he was playing on Eddie's mobile to look up.

She saw Stan, his face as excited as her brother's on Christmas morning.

"Ready?" she heard Wes ask her. She turned to answer him and saw that he was pushing down his hood without anyone telling him to, setting his spikes of white-blond hair free.

It was a brave, bold move for a shy, strange boy.

Maybe it was time Kiki got brave too.

"Just a sec," she whispered to Wes, and then leaned into the mic.

"Hi, I'm Kiki and this is my friend Wes," Kiki began, her voice a little wobbly as she heard it amplified. "Before we do our song, I, um, just wanted to say something..."

She heard a warning cough coming from the

direction of Mrs Evans at the side of the stage. She ignored it.

"Starting secondary school is exciting and a bit scary. You're going to meet a whole load of new people," said Kiki. "You might find brilliant new friends, or you might find people who *feel* like friends at first, but aren't really. People who don't make you feel good about yourself."

Kiki paused, wondering if Lola was still in the hall or not, and realizing she didn't care.

"But because everything is so new and confusing, you might not figure out who's who for a while. So take your time and get to know lots of people, cos your best friends might end up being people you don't even notice at first."

Kiki stopped there, giddy with the relief of speaking up, giddy with the freedom of not being trapped in the cage of Lola's crew any more.

"Er, thank you," she said, suddenly shy as a wave of applause rippled towards the stage.

"Thank you, Kiki!" said Mrs Evans, coming over to join her. "Very sensible advice there! Now, how about we hear some music from you and—"

The packed hall was suddenly plunged into a

twilight darkness, the overhead lights and the huge screen snuffed out.

For a split second, all Kiki could make out was a sickly green tinge to the blackening sky outside – that and the glowing dart of a lightsabre in among the shadowy audience.

Then the lightning strike hit hard. Outside, the force of it illuminated the playground; inside, the hall trembled and shook.

For a moment, there was just shocked silence, then the panic began.

WES: One missing Ty

The overhead lights powered back on, but flickered, playing a will-they-go-off-again game of cat and mouse with the startled audience.

An audience that was rapidly leaving, empty seats dotting the rows. Including Stan's, Wes noticed. Where had he gone?

"Well, it looks as if we might have another unexpected storm on our hands!" Mrs Evans tried to say calmly – even jokily – into the mic, above the racket of the rain now lashing against the hall windows. "But just in case there's been some structural damage to the building, I think it's best if everyone makes their way out calmly and safely..."

Wes screeched his chair back as Mrs Evans hurried past him. She trotted quickly down the steps from the stage, off to help other members of staff guide the tide of parents, carers and Year Six kids as they streamed up the aisles and disappeared through the doors at the back of the hall.

Wes got up, put his drums on the chair and saw that Kiki was stuck, her hair caught in the strap of her ukulele in her hurry to take it off over her head.

"Here," he said, trying to tug free the tangle of dark curls at the nape of her neck.

"What's happening, Wes?" Kiki asked, tilting her head to the side, her eyes on the churning skies outside. "Is this it? Have the rescuers come for Stan? Is he gone? I can't see him!"

"I can't see him either," said Wes, his trembling fingers finally working the strands of hair loose. "But this *can't* be a rescue mission, Kiki! Stan said they'd be professional and calm and come in the middle of the night. And anyway, they wouldn't be able to find him – Stan's destroyed the location alerter. He showed me."

Kiki flipped round to face Wes.

"He's *what*? But how will he get home?"

"He won't. He doesn't want to. He wants to stay here on Earth," said Wes, helping lift the ukulele strap over his startled friend's head and laying the instrument on top of his drums.

"So do you think it's his classmates, the Others, come to look for Stan?" suggested Kiki.

"The weather's weird enough for it to be them," said Wes. "But if they were trying to rescue him, why would they be messing around making storms?"

"Because they're idiots?" said Kiki. "That's pretty much what Stan's said about them, isn't it? I wish he was here to tell us what's going on. Where do you think he went?"

"I guess he could've gone to the basement," said Wes. "To hide or recharge or—"

"C'mon, guys! Let's go!" they both heard Mr McKenzie call out from the back of the hall.

Wes felt Kiki's hand reaching for his as they made their own way off the stage and began to run down the near-deserted hall, Mr McKenzie urging them to get a move on.

Along with the last of the stragglers, they bundled out of the double entrance doors into the wet slap of the wind. Wes glanced up at the roof of the school, but it seemed intact after the lightning strike.

"So should we sneak off to the basement and

see if Stan's there?" Wes suggested, as the storm bustled and boomed overhead, with brittle, chilled darts of water hammering down on them.

"I want to, but Mum will be worrying," said Kiki, glancing around while she took her phone out of her blazer pocket. Almost immediately, it jangled into life.

"Hi, Mum! Yeah, no, don't worry. I'm with my friend Wes. Where are you?"

Kiki's volume was up loud, so Wes heard enough of the muffled response to work out what was happening. Kiki's mum was in the street, helping a cyclist who'd just skidded off his bike and might have fractured something. She was going to stay with him till an ambulance came. Eddie and Ty were somewhere in the playground, waiting for Kiki.

"OK, I'll find them," Kiki assured her mum. "I'll check in with you later. Bye!"

Wes was already turning this way and that, dampness soaking through his jacket and chilling him to the bone. All he saw was the thinning trickle of people filing out of the main gate. There was no one left in the main playground and no sign of Ty or Eddie.

"Where are they?" Kiki asked.

And then Wes saw it – the glint of something; a long, glowing shard of white light dipping and bobbing down in the lower playground. "Look!"

"That's Ty! That's his lightsabre!" said Kiki, immediately breaking into a run that was interrupted by another jangle from her phone.

Wes saw the name Eddie on the display before Kiki lifted it to her ear.

"Eddie! What are you and Ty doing down in the lower playground?" she yelled.

"I'm not there – I'm out in the street, looking for Ty," Wes heard Eddie's voice say urgently. "He just bolted on me!"

"Why would he do that?" Kiki asked, confused.

"I don't know… He said he'd seen something on my phone," Eddie babbled.

Kiki shook her head, as if it would help her think straight. But Ty wasn't safe on his own in the dark, in the storm, in a place where rogue aliens might be trying to find their classmate. Wes grabbed the phone from Kiki.

"Hi, it's Wes – can you run down to the river and go along the path there?" he asked Eddie.

"I'm right by my motorbike – that'll be quicker," said Eddie. "But what do you want me to do when I get there?"

"Look for a tear in the fence," Wes carried on, already hearing the growl of the engine. "You can climb through the hole into the lower playground. We're heading there now, and if you come in that way, we'll have Ty cornered."

"Sure – I'm on it," said Eddie, then the connection went dead.

While Wes had slowed to talk, Kiki had kept on running.

"TY! TY!" she was shouting, though the wind did its best to snatch her words away.

Ahead of his friend, Wes saw a fluttering gleam of silvery yellow in the dark sprawl of the bushes as the wind buffeted their branches back and forth.

The pod's invisibility shield – it was malfunctioning again!

Wes looked up at the sky, knowing the best view of the faulty craft was from up there.

Uh-oh...

STAR BOY: Danger on high

The Others were back.

Not a rescue mission moving stealthily and effectively in the deep of night, but irresponsible Others barrelling into the Earth's atmosphere, causing mayhem once again.

The Star Boy sat in his pod, listening intently to the faint and fluttering communication device. He heard the Others jabbering among themselves and quickly he understood. Earth satellites had been monitored, and with no Human sightings of him reported, the Star Boy was presumed dead.

The Others had come here illicitly, sneaking the pods off base and planning their own mission – to seek out and destroy any evidence of the Star Boy and his craft. They hoped to impress the Master with their ingenuity. It might have been a noble plan, except for the fact that they STILL couldn't resist playing around with laser bolts and Earth clouds.

As he listened to his former classmates' chatter and tutted at their wilfulness, the Star Boy suddenly noticed the soft, silent blip of an orange light on the control panel. All three of his hearts began to race.

It was such a small, insignificant light. Such a pretty colour. Yet it meant something catastrophic. The erratic invisibility shield had just switched itself off again. It meant that the pod would be *gleamingly* visible from the sky. Any second now, one of the Others would spot it, lock their lasers on and obliterate it – without realizing *the Star Boy was inside*.

He scrambled out of the pod. The Star Boy's craft, and the greenery it was hidden inside, would be turned to ash at any moment. He needed to get as far away as he could before—

"HELLO!" said the Young Human, as the Star Boy burst out of the bushes.

It was Kiki's brother, who had asked so many questions when they'd met at Kiki's home the day before. His name was 'Ty', the Star Boy recalled.

And Ty was holding the torch-like item that the Star Boy had seen Kiki wave around the first night he'd ever set alien eyes on her. The child's chest seemed rounder than he remembered, till he saw that it was a bag, worn at the front instead of the back, as others wore them.

"I KNOW what's in there!" Ty announced, pointing his white torchlight at the tall, dense shrubs. "I saw it on the drone footage on Eddie's phone just now! You know my sister! How come YOU'VE been in there? Have you seen it too?"

The Star Boy stared at the talkative child. He knew it was polite to answer questions, but there was no time right now, not with danger lurking on high in the grumbling clouds. He needed to act with great speed, and so did the only logical thing he could.

"HELLLLPPP!" Ty yelped in surprise, as he found himself lifted off his feet and thrown over the Star Boy's shoulder, hurtled round the perimeter of the bushes and shuffled through the creaking, clanking hole in the fence where, close by, the roaring, racing River Wouze whirled itself into a frenzy, mirroring the wildness of the skies above.

"TY! STAN!" The Star Boy heard the wind-whipped voice of his friend Kiki call out.

"We are here!" he called back, barely feeling the small fists pummelling his back and the feet kicking his belly, or the hard lump of the rucksack pressing against his shoulder blades.

"KIKI! I'M BEING KIDNAPPED!" Ty roared very loudly for someone upside down.

The Star Boy was relieved to see both Kiki and Wes wriggle their way between the bushes and the wire fence.

"What's happening?" Kiki gasped, as she slipped through the gap in the wire, followed by Wes. "What are you doing with Ty?"

The Star Boy's energy was dipping. He was struggling to remain Morphed, his amber self beginning to glow.

"It is the Others – they mean to strike and destroy the pod!" he shouted, his words practically swallowed by the roar of the river, and another growling sound he didn't recognize.

"They can see it, can't they?" Wes asked, clearly understanding the danger as he gazed up at the sky and the ominous flecks of yellow light within the clouds.

"Yes – we must evacuate this area immediately!" the Star Boy urged them, though he was concerned that they might not be able to leave fast enough to guarantee safety.

And then a strange, deafeningly loud Human vehicle roared along the riverside path and screeched to a halt beside them.

The young Human Man was driving it; the Star Boy knew him to be the person who wasn't Kiki's mother yesterday, as Wes had explained this to him as they left. His head was encased in a round red ball.

"You found him!" said Eddie, pushing up a plastic sheet on the front of the ball. "But what's going on?"

Eddie's smile faded as he looked at the growing amber glow of the Star Boy's skin.

Like Ty, he appeared to be on the verge of asking many questions, but there was even less time for this now. All that mattered was that the noisy, odd-shaped vehicle was the *only* way the Star Boy could get his friends out of here alive.

"We need to leave on this craft now – the element of danger is at a critical point!" he yelled at Kiki and Wes.

"No way! I don't have room," Eddie protested. "And it's illegal and –"

"– and we might DIE if we don't hurry!" Kiki shouted, glancing up at the broiling mustard-green sky. "DO IT!"

The Star Boy noticed Eddie following her gaze. The sharp dots of light in the cloud above their heads were zipping about in an agitated state, like wasps about to sting.

"Whoa..." Eddie muttered.

"Exactly," said Kiki, who was helping the Star Boy get into the bubble-shaped sidecar, and plonking Ty on his lap, along with the child's long torch and bag. The Star Boy was impressed by her speed and efficiency as she now pushed Wes on to the main vehicle behind Eddie, before she herself jumped on behind *him*, all three crushed and clinging together in a row.

"GO!" Kiki shouted, and they screeched off along the riverside path, turning on to the pedestrian bridge, just as the most awful noise burst out behind them.

The Star Boy – still holding firm to the now

gobsmacked Ty – spun round and witnessed several blasts of neon-yellow bolts detonating, the first a direct hit to the Wouze. A hard slap of river water cascaded over the passengers and their transport, causing them all to gasp with cold and fear.

As they bumpily exited the far side of the bridge, the Star Boy heard Wes's shocked voice.

"It's on fire – the school's on fire!"

The last hope hideout

KIKI: No place like home

The overloaded motorbike and sidecar didn't pass a soul as it puttered across the high street and up the hill towards the Electrical Emporium.

The townspeople of Fairfield were all safely indoors, and if anyone had happened to look out of their window, it would be to wonder at the sound of the freakish 'lightning strikes' and the distant whine of fire-engine sirens – not at the hunched figures zipping by on the rickety vehicle.

And now those same figures were safely indoors themselves. Once Eddie had parked the motorbike in the darkened yard of his shop, they'd all stumbled through the rear door of the building and into the back room of the Emporium. Kiki gazed round at what appeared to be a workshop, living room and kitchen combined, cosily lit by several old-fashioned, fringed table lamps and garlands of fairy lights, all with a smattering of popped bulbs. Eddie's own collection of random treasures that other people would've dumped...

"Hello? Mum?"

Kiki's phone rang as soon as she slumped exhausted on a squashy sofa, Wes by her side. Stan and Ty were on the other sofa, while Eddie hovered awkwardly, uncertain what to do or how to act with an unexpected alien visitor in his home.

"No, honestly, we're all right. We were halfway up the hill before the lightning hit, so we didn't see anything," Kiki lied to her mum. "Only the buildings in the lower playground were damaged? And you're sure no one got hurt? Oh good..."

Glad as she was for the news update from Mum, Kiki was desperate to end the call – she needed to find out from Stan that he *really* was fine, now the possibility of returning to his planet was gone. She needed to check that Eddie was doing OK after finding himself a getaway driver during an alien attack. She needed Ty to stop poking Stan with his finger.

"So your bus is just coming? OK, Mum, yes … see you when you get back. Bye!" she said cheerfully, while leaning over and pulling her brother's arm away.

"I just wanted to see what he's MADE of!" Ty protested. "He doesn't mind, DO you!"

Stan shook his gently glowing head.

"Hey, Stan, do you think there's a chance that the Others will come back?" Wes asked.

"All evidence of my existence is gone, so they have no reason to return," Stan replied.

"Are you talking about your SPACESHIP getting trashed?" Ty said excitedly, jumping up on to his knees and starting to bounce. "I saw it, didn't I? I saw it in the DRONE FOOTAGE on Eddie's phone and then I saw it FOR REAL in the bushes in the playground. And I saw aliens flying in the sky AGES ago, but NO ONE believed me!"

Kiki saw Stan flinching at the endless loud babble.

"Ty, shush," she said. "And please stop bouncing – you'll make Stan sick."

"But I need to KNOW stuff!" Ty insisted, his eyes locked on Stan. "Like what your ALIEN SUPERPOWER is, and how aliens go to the TOILET, and why your hands have started to look so WEIRD!"

Ty grabbed Stan's limp arm; the Morphing was fading faster, the fingers changing to the fin shapes Kiki had first seen in the music room, when Stan had sneezily materialized in front of her and Wes.

"Leave him alone!" Kiki scolded her brother, getting up to untangle him from Stan. He wriggled and protested as she took him back to her own seat and held him tightly on her lap.

"Look, I, er, don't really understand what's going on here, but your friend doesn't look very well," said Eddie.

Kiki had to give him credit: Eddie might be completely bamboozled, but he was still being pretty cool in the circumstances. And caring too. Stan did look worn out.

"I am very tired," said Stan.

"He needs to recharge," Wes added urgently.

Kiki turned to Eddie. "Stan needs electricity ... quite a *lot* of electricity. Can you help him?"

"Uh, OK, sure. That's an emergency generator I hire out for wedding marquees and stuff," said Eddie, pointing to the big metal box that his small TV was sitting on top of. "It's fully charged.

Will it do?"

Practically before Eddie got to the end of his sentence, Stan had stumbled off the sofa and loped over to the box. With a grateful sigh, he slid down to the floor with his back against it, elemental pulses of neon yellow beginning to aura around him.

At that same moment, the jukebox in the next room burst into life, blasting out an old rock 'n' roll song. The TV switched itself on too, showing some random advert for toothpaste, before it promptly blacked out with a sizzle of smoke drifting from the top of it.

"Sorry if I am surging," Stan apologized, sparks dotting round his fin-shaped hands. "I am very depleted."

"It's ... it's fine – I can fix that," said Eddie, bending down to unplug the TV.

Kiki couldn't hold Ty still any longer, and he wriggled free.

"That was BRILLIANT! Do something ELSE, alien!" he demanded, hunkering down on the floor beside Stan.

"Watch – I can do *this*!" said Stan, blinking side to side and earning delighted whoops from Ty.

Kiki smiled, glad to see the Star Boy's brightness returning. But she still needed to ask him a serious question.

"Stan – Wes told me about you destroying the location alerter," she said, leaning forwards on the sofa. "Are you all right with that? Not being able to go back to your home planet?"

"I am happy, of course!" Stan announced emphatically. "Now I have no fear of discovery, I can dedicate myself to researching all there is to know about the Earth and its marvels. For example, did you know that my pigeons will have flown off to safety *before* the laser strike? Just before storms or dangerous weather events happen, Earth birds and other animals can detect subtle changes in barometric pressure and also react to infrasound – or sound at a frequency too low for Humans to hear – and so remove themselves to shelter and safety. Is that not *fascinating*?"

Kiki and Wes stared at the fact-babbling Star Boy.

"Yeah, he's right, actually. I read that," said Eddie, as if he was having a nice chat with an interesting new friend and not a stray and stranded alien.

"I LOVE having an alien friend!" Ty announced.

"Can I give you a HUG?"

"Nope, not unless you fancy an electric shock," said Eddie, grabbing Ty and keeping him safe, just like he so often did, Kiki had to admit.

"Well, can I SHOW my alien something then?" Ty asked, and scampered off across the room before anyone could reply.

"I'd say he'll calm down once he gets used to you, but that would be a lie," Kiki told Stan.

"But hold on – how's this going to work?" said Wes, his white eyebrows bent into a frown. "Stan isn't going to be able to go back to the boiler room if the building's been damaged."

"I guess ... I guess he could hide out here," suggested Eddie, running his hands through his hair. "Just till the school building is sorted, I mean. How does that sound, er, Stan?"

"Yes! That is very acceptable! Thank you!" Stan said in delight.

Kiki felt a wave of guilt, knowing that she'd always thought of Eddie as a slightly annoying goofball, when all the time he'd just been kind and nice, simple as that. She definitely needed to work more on the whole giving-people-a-chance thing.

And she would, now that she was morphing back to the old version of Kiki, the kinder Kiki she'd been before she became friends with Lola and the toxic Popular Crew...

"SURPRISE!" roared Ty, jumping back down in front of Stan, pulling something out of his backpack, and thrusting the orange exercise ball pretty much in Stan's face.

From what Kiki understood so far, the Star Boy came from a civilization that was used to an environment and technology more sophisticated and advanced than anything anyone on Earth could ever properly imagine.

But one thing they clearly weren't used to was hamsters.

"AAAAA-EEEEEEE!" screeched Stan.

"*Squeak!*" squeaked Squeak.

POP! went several fairy lights, as Stan surged with the shock.

"Teaching him to be a human could be complicated," Wes said under his breath to Kiki.

It certainly could, thought Kiki.

And she just couldn't wait to start.

**Can't wait for
the next book?
Turn the page for
a sneaky peek...**

The best kept secret in town

The people of the small town of Fairfield hadn't a clue. After the strange and unexpected storms of the last few weeks, they were glad that everything seemed nearly back to normal. As far as they were concerned, it was an ordinary, sleepy Sunday. The weather was playing nicely, with nothing more dramatic happening than a chilly breeze teasing the autumn leaves on the trees, trying to tempt them to come for a spin.

In the park, parents chatted as their children played, discussing the freak lightning bolt that had struck Riverside Academy during its Open Evening last Thursday, all the while gazing across the river at the building and marvelling that no one had been hurt. Only the sight of several heavily-laden lorries trundling through the park gates, ready to set up for the annual funfair, diverted their attention away with conversation turning to plans for outings and fun on the rides.

Down by the River Wouse, teenagers slouched on the railings and gawped across the water at the shattered windows of their school and the huge hazard-taped crater in the lower playground. Passing gum around, they wondered about seeing the new blockbuster movie tomorrow, since school would be closed for at least one more day, hopefully more.

Wherever they were and whatever they were doing, the entire population of Fairfield – almost – were clueless about the mind-blowing visitor hidden away, right under their noses. Or up at the shabby little parade of shops on the north side of town, to be precise.

In between the old-fashioned laundrette, and the faded grocers shop, the Electrical Emporium practically glowed with the secret stashed in its back room.

A back room that was a messy muddle of things: a work space where the temperamental kettles, toasters and PlayStations of Fairfield were fixed; a cosy living room, with reams of semi-working fairy lights looped and dangling across every wall; a kitchen, with a gurgling fridge and a sink full of often-forgotten dishes.

And since the supposed 'lightning strike', it had become a safe haven for a homeless alien. A Star Boy, stranded far, far from his solar system.

But there was one thing the residents of Fairfield had in common with the stowed-away Star Boy. *None* of them had an inkling about the urgent mission being planned on a faraway planet. A mission to rescue the lost alien – who didn't *technically* want to be found.

Or that the spacecraft and its crew were scheduled to arrive around teatime next Saturday...

Tuesday:
How to hide
a homeless
alien

STAR BOY:
A glimpse of what was gone

The Star Boy scrolled through the data lens in his left eye.

"Seven million, six hundred and thirty two thousand seconds," he announced as he crouched on the moth-eaten rug in the back room of the Electrical Emporium, staring at the four Humans in front of him: the tall girl (Kiki), the short boy (Wes), the child (Ty) and the young man (Eddie).

"What are you on about?" asked his friend – and rescuer – Kiki.

"I fell to Earth seven million, six hundred and thirty two thousand seconds ago," explained the Star Boy happily.

"You mean *ten* days ago?" suggested Wes, his other friend and rescuer. "That's how people would say it. And you've been here at Eddie's for three days."

"Ah, yes, I understand," murmured the Star Boy. He found the dazzling array of Human descriptions for time both baffling and fascinating. It could be talked about as seconds or minutes or hours. Days and nights could be split into categories such as 'dawn' and 'dusk' and 'lunchtime'.

Still, what surprised the Star Boy about his calculation was that he almost expected it to be longer. So very, *very* much had happened. And *all* of it had been thrilling. The crashing, the hiding, the learning, the wonder, the joy, the fear of the last ten days – as well as learning to Morph into a passable Human. But it had resulted in an enormous drain on his energy reserves.

Unable to return to the basement of Fairfield Academy and the comforting Danger! Box energy source, the Star Boy had been glad and grateful when Kiki and Wes had smuggled him to the safety of this higgledy-piggledy back room. He'd barely moved from the small generator he'd been relieved to find in it. Throughout the days and hours and minutes and seconds, the Star Boy had dipped in and out of blankness as he recharged, his entire skin-covering glowing amber, and gently vibrating with the electricity that pulsed through his luminous body.

Sometimes he'd become conscious and find himself alone, taking the chance then to explore his immediate surroundings. He'd wander the room, perhaps poking soft squares called cushions, maybe opening drawers and stroking silver pointed implements called forks. He'd even tried poking the cushions with the forks, which he'd found quite fun.

Sometimes he'd be quietly recharging while Eddie – owner of the Electrical Emporium and repairer of broken things – went about his business, with a wave and a quick 'All right?'. The Star Boy watched as Eddie repaired items with a hot metal wand called a soldering iron, threw brown orbs called Maltesers in the air, catching them – miraculously – in his mouth, and made crick-cricking noises in his nose when he fell asleep in front of the TV.

And then sometimes, the Star Boy would rise to consciousness and be joyful to find Kiki and Wes by his side. The small Human too – the little brother of Kiki.

Like now.

"I think I would like to show you all something. Something from before the last ten days!" the Star Boy announced, in the English of his rescuers.

Ty bounced on the sofa beside Kiki. "Are you going to show us your alien SUPERPOWER?" he asked excitedly.

Kiki shushed her brother as the Star Boy turned and stared intently at the inky black screen of the TV that was balanced on top of the generator.

"Sorry, but what exactly are you trying to do, Stan?" Kiki asked, using the Human name they'd settled on calling him. The Star Boy liked it. He felt happy to be known as 'Stan'; 'Stan Boyd', in fact. All of his life so far, the Star Boy had simply been referred to as a long line of unmemorable code.

"I am attempting to download visual information from my data lens onto this primitive machine," the Star Boy explained, his intense concentration causing crackles to ignite inside and across his chest.

During discussions and comparisons of their respective worlds, the Star Boy found he had not been able to adequately describe what his everyday environment *looked* like, but just this minute he'd hit upon the idea of transmuting images of its constant and dazzling electrical brightness onto the TV.

"What sort of 'visual information'? What are you going to show us, Stan?" Wes asked next.

"My home," the Star Boy said simply.

Though nothing was simple about what had happened. His home was no longer his home. It was lost to him, gone, he'd never return. And the Star Boy was glad of it. Terrifying as it had been, he was glad that the Others had come – under cover of rumbling storm clouds and darkness – and lasered his stricken craft to ashes, presuming him dead, hoping to hide all evidence of his existence.

But he was far from dead. In fact, the Star Boy had never felt more alive than he did now. Alive, and experiencing something *no* other Star Boy ever had. And it was only fair that he show his wonderful Humans a glimpse of a sight never before witnessed by *their* species.

Kiki and Wes.

Ty and Eddie.

Already he felt more of a kinship with this mismatching collection of Humans than with anyone back on his planet, where the concept of having